Eddie Johnson's Ark

A lumberyard tale for those of us under construction.

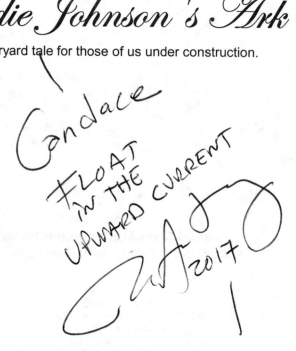

Candace
FLOAT IN THE UPWARD CURRENT
2017

by **Ross Anthony**

To Gramma Jennie with love

www.RossAnthony.com/books
For other Books, Essays & Articles by Ross Anthony

"Eddie Johnson's Ark"
Copyright © 1997-2006 by Ross Anthony at Arizona Blueberry Studios
© Cover Art by Ross Anthony – Photo of Ross by Ken Kocanda
Edited by R. Foss, K. Kocanda, I. Huang. J. Keszek.
Special Thanks
Ingrid, Ken, Rick, Terry, Philip & Fay, Jodie

For other Arizona Blueberry books go to:
www.RossAnthony.com/books
ISBN 0-9727894-2-1   ISBN13: 978-0-9727894-24
First Printing 1/2004
10 9 8 7 6 5   1500 11/05

Day -15

The evening sun slips into the dents and hardware scratches that hold together Eddie's reliable old pickup truck. A lone two-by-four bumps and skips in the bed, making a few new scrapes. Eddie rubs his tired eyes, then sneezes abruptly, barely getting his hands in front of his face in time to keep the snot and sawdust from hitting the windshield. The sneeze turns into a yawn as he jabs callused stubby fingers blindly at the radio tuner, keeping a dusty eye on the crowded road. The traffic light ahead turns bloodshot red.

Radio: "...But a little cooler for the evening. Don't put that grill away yet, looks like another clear weekend for the greater Columbus metropolitan area following yet another hot and dry work week. And that's it for the weather on the ones ...now for..." **click**: "... the mayor still denies any involvement ..." **click** "... the drought. Farmers in other Midwestern States have already extended loans ..." **click** ... Paul Simon's "For Emily" plays:

> ... And when I awoke
> And felt you warm and near
> I kissed your honey hair
> With my grateful tears ...

The light changes to green. The group of cars and trucks and buses move a block or so like sheep in a corral to the next yellow, now red light. They stop, again, in unison.

An old bearded man, catching a glimpse of Eddie through the dirty windshield, hops to his feet from his newspaper bed on the bus stop bench. His leap implies some sort of instinct or plain-as-day knowledge that Eddie is going to be good for a quarter. As the sound of milk poured in a bowl cracks the eye of a sleeping cat, the sight of Eddie enlivens the empty-pocketed old man. Wrinkled and gray to the point of cabbage and cotton, the man jumps to life, grabs his squeegee and slaps it across Eddie's gritty windshield.

Eddie grimaces, the lights change, cars drive around him like ants around squashed brethren. With a sigh, Eddie fiddles his fingers through the ashtray, then his pockets, rounding up only a dime and a few pennies. With one eye on the old man, he secretly checks his wallet for a small bill. It's empty save for a ten and a five, and a picture of his late wife Emily.

Glancing back at the change, Eddie grunts, rolls down the window and slides the cabbage-patch man the five-dollar bill. The brisk wind of such generosity trips the old man into a backward stumble. Holding the bill up happily, he waves it at Eddie. Eddie's grumbling momentarily breaks into a brief smile before he sighs and turns onto the highway.

The radio's melody changes, finding only half an ear on Eddie's head. On the opposite side of Eddie's head and the highway, emergency crews are all over a multiple car accident. Blue, red, and white lights strobe and reflect off the tops of four lanes of vehicular standstill. In Eddie's direction, the leftmost two lanes slow and nearly stop, populated by gapers. Eddie speeds along in the right lane, ignoring the mars lights, sirens and luring wreckage. With three sons, he'll find enough wreckage when he gets home.

Day -14

A scalding bone-dry breeze swirls the sawdust in a remote corner of JJ's Lumberyard. The wood chips swarm like bees in a miniature tornado. Three sweat-covered lumber workers crank and tighten the last few bolts on a sparkling orange forklift so new that the parched wooden planks nearby seem to bend upwards with its mere presence.

Joe Stacey oils its chain, checks his watch and tosses the pump can in his toolbox all in one motion, "Quittin' time, I'm outta here." His expression hasn't varied since noon.

Eddie Johnson, a large bear of a man, down on one knee, finishes his cranking, drops the wrench and screwdriver in his tool box. He stands, gazes up at the crusty setting sun through blank eyes, sweat, and the sawdust in his hair, then with a heavy sigh, he ambles toward the pickup.

David MacMay, the last of the three yard workers, looks up from the machine to see his coworkers on their way to clock out. His jaw drops open, his young green eyes widen, he shouts at their backs, "What? You gotta be kiddin'? We spent all afternoon puttin' it together and you ain't even gonna..." Their indifference stops him mid-sentence, he lowers his voice, "...take it for a spin?"

Eddie leans to the left compensating for the weight of the tools hanging from his right hand grip. Without breaking his stride, he tosses the keys to the forklift over his shoulder to David.

JJ Hayle sits in his kiosk office littered with newspapers, coffee cups and doughnut crumbs. He's wearing two pieces of a three-piece pinstriped suit – the jacket is hanging on the door. Leaning back on a leather office chair with both legs straight out and crossed, feet up on the desk, he's unabashedly amused by the latest TV news story.

Eddie and Joe step into the kiosk, slip their gritty cards through the time clock and turn to leave. Neither bats an eye at JJ's inviting smile. "Look at this, Johnson," JJ barks, "Some guy cuts his wife up with a can opener."

Eddie raises his eyebrows as a courtesy, but doesn't slow his step out the door. JJ stares in amusement at Eddie's dramatic lack of interest; the smoke from JJ's cigarette leaks out of his stool-eating smile. JJ yells out at him, "A fucking can opener! Can you believe that?"

Eddie rubs his sore neck and tosses the toolbox in the back of his twenty-year-old pickup while Joe peels off in his decked out rig – complete with light rack, bra and all the other trimmings that went out of style fifteen years ago. Joe had to special order them and Eddie had to listen to him whine about their costs everyday until they arrived.

Eddie fires up the engine, glancing at David in the rearview mirror giddily making circles in the dirt, riding the splendid orange forklift like a cowboy.

Bill Battlon pauses his cleaning to peek out the spotless nine-foot picture window of his Doughnuts & Burger Grill which rests catty-corner to the lumberyard. He squints his eyes disapprovingly at David's childishness.

Eddie pulls away, flips on the radio: "…said he was quiet and stand-offish. Thomas is held without bail, the wife's mother said that she'd like to see the can opener used to carve a hole in his…" **click** "…setting fire to a nearby orphanage, all but three…" **click**

The approaching light turns red. Eddie's truck slows and stops. Two cars behind, a man scrambles to a late model SUV. He grabs open the driver's side door and forcibly ejects the woman driving. The woman stumbles to the curb as the man drives off in her car. The event is out of Eddie's view, but those in clear eye-shot stare straight ahead, redirecting their adrenaline into cowardly hopes that they won't be involved.

Eddie's drive home drones in redundancy to the drive home the day before and the day before and the day before. The radio's on, the horns are blaring; but Eddie fades back into thoughts of better days, when the kids were young and his wife was alive. In a daydream instant, the thirty-minute drive is over and Eddie pulls up to a modest bungalow.

Japeth, Eddie's nine-year-old son, sits on the couch motionless, save for his nimble thumbs nearing a blur of bustle atop his handheld video game. If not for the glare across his glasses, the precision scrambling of his pupils would also be visible.

Henry, Eddie's seventeen-year-old, scratches a number two pencil against his forehead, pulling at some pubescent facial hair near his ears and on his chin. He sighs and checks his calculations in the back of the book. He wasn't even close. The house is humble, yet exceptional, "Eddie & sons" handiwork abound. Wood at every turn, fresh one-by-eights running the length of most walls. Oak chairs with thick lathed legs. A gorgeous mahogany door welcomes guests on the wraparound front porch, over which a swing gently sways in the arid breeze. If any member of the family ever had to say, "Knock on wood" they wouldn't have to reach far to do it. All the wood is sanded, solid and cleverly functional. Eddie's no genius -- he can't play piano, jeopardy or quote Shakespeare, but he sure as timber knows how to handle wood.

Henry rubs what's left of the worn eraser across his homework; the numbers smear more than erase. The TV is on in front of him, but he doesn't look up at it.

TV: "…crews are still working feverishly to contain the blaze. They are tired and overworked. Authorities say if the next fire break doesn't do it, they'll be forced to let nature

take its course in the park, like the fire that burned Yellowstone at the end of the last millennium."

Eddie treads in, carefully closing that huge mahogany door, flicking off the TV on his way to the kitchen. Japeth makes no notice of him, and kills a squadron of aliens with four thumb strokes. Henry, still erasing: "Dad??? I was watching that!"

Already in the kitchen, Eddie hasn't any intention of responding to Henry. Sam, Eddie's fifteen-year-old, nods 'hello' while reading the directions in a crusty and burnt cookbook. A pot of rice and water on the stove starts to boil over. Eddie lowers the flame.

Sam looks up, "Thanks dad."

Eddie makes his way to the restroom, putting his big hands on Sam's narrow shoulders as he passes. Door closed behind him, Eddie takes a seat on the commode. He reaches into his back pocket (on the floor) and pulls out his wallet to study a photo of Emily. Trousers down, crouched forward, he grabs a wad of toilet paper and sneezes out some more sawdust.

Meanwhile, in the kitchen, donning a pair of potholder mittens, Sam reaches into the oven and pulls out a surprisingly decent-looking roast. His pride perks, accompanied by a savory anticipation of an unburned dinner (for a change).

Japeth wanders into the kitchen still banging on the video game. He mumbles, "Chef Samster... What's Jeanie gonna do when you guys get married, fix the car?"

"Look, game boy, If you don't wanna starve, you might think about shuttin' up and settin' the table!" Sam responds in his big brother voice.

Eddie flushes and steps into the shower. Cool water runs down his dusty body like the Nile through Egypt. He coughs and inhales the moisture, holding a breath of calm as

this bathroom-contained sunshower of peace rinses away all the soot and garbage from beard to toe.

Having set out the dishes and forks, Henry and Japeth sit hungrily at the table. Henry, happy to put away the math; Japeth, still slamming silently at his electronic toy. Eddie steps out of the john with a Q-tip hanging from his ear.

Sam's eyes point at the Q-tip, "Uh, dad."

Eddie finishes cleaning that ear and tosses the filthy cotton swab into the garbage. He then helps Sam serve the proud feast. The two join Japeth and Henry at the table. Just as three Johnson family members raise their forks to chow down, they are simultaneously stopped at the sound of Henry saying grace. The mouthwatering aroma of food wafts imperviously, as Henry, eyes closed, hands folded, softly gives thanks. The pause of the fork-fisted Johnsons is not one of respect -- just distraction; they realize their mistake and once again chomp down hard into the roast and rice.

Henry continues his prayer meditatively till finished, then opens his eyes to see his family guiltlessly indulging and shamelessly ignoring him. First silently scornful, then somewhat embarrassed for his unwelcome chant, he joins them in the dinner.

All is silent save open mouth chewing and the occasional burp. A pigeon on the windowsill goes unnoticed.

At JJ's penthouse, forty-five stories above street level, a pigeon on the windowsill goes unnoticed.

JJ, too, digs into his dinner. The apartment is far too art déco for his personal doing, he'd paid the last condo owner an extra twenty grand to "leave all this pretty shit here." He's on the phone, dining alone, fork in one hand, TV clicker in the other. Scanning the news, pouring a messy jar of spaghetti sauce over his rotini, JJ chews, holding his cellular phone between his ear and shoulder, "Yeah, Yeah, a

fuckin' can opener. Yeah." He swallows, "No shit? Who? Richardson?" He looks down at the table, "Hold on."

JJ shuts off the TV, takes another forkful of pasta, clicks the wireless phone and dials a number: "Larry baby, JJ," all smiles now, "we're gonna have ta delay dat transfer ah Girl Scout cookies." JJ grins, "Yeah, som'in' like dat. We gotta sick den-mommy to replace," nods, "Dat'll work. Yo."

JJ squints his eyes at the little phone and mumbles to himself, "Where the hell's that goddamn flash button... Oh," he clicks the button, "Great ace, I've got a bowl a s'getti starin' me in the face here ... Yeah, yeah, yeah, ya gonna let me finish my goddamn pasta or what?"

The pigeon dives from the sill into the street below.

David stands in his sparsely furnished home. He's at the dinner table setting his baby daughter Sheila into her high chair. Sue, his wife, blows the hair out of her eyes as she sets the food out and takes her seat with a sigh.

"Good broccolis, damn good broccolis!" David smiles toward Sue. Sue responds with a somber hard face. David counters by picking up a piece of meat with his fingers and bringing it to Sheila's mouth, "Good pork chops hmm? Sheila? Can you say pork chops? ... Pooorrrkkkk Cchoppss."

David's giddiness prompts Sue to burst into tears.

"Babe?" David's eyes widen, he turns his head to Sue, "Ah, don't do that... Come on, what is it?" Then barely audibly, "...now?"

"They called again." Sue speaks bravely through the sniffling.

"They? They who? They who called?"

"You know!" She stands, "Those goddamn creditors!" then runs into the kitchen to hide her face, or more accurately, hide from David's face. Defeating her, David gets up and follows her into the kitchen.

"Jesus!" David is oblivious to the outside world, "I've been at the same job for over a year. What's with those guys?"

Sheila chomps blissfully alone, her indifferent silhouette contrasting the half million pixels comprising a full color 27-inch television set. The news plays, but the volume is too low to be heard.

"They don't care, David. They said they'll just wait till you leave tomorrow, waltz right in here and take the TV."

"They can't do that."

"David, wake up 'n' smell the coffee. Have you noticed the washing machine around here for the past week? We're sinkin', honey. We're goin' under."

"I'm workin' now babe. I haven't missed that many days at the yard. They like me there. I'm doin' okay."

"I know, Davie. I know." She sighs, regaining her composure. "It's just not enough. We're sinkin'. I've been tryin' to tell you, explain the accounts to you, but you're so damn hardheaded!"

Sue chokes on her next thought, "And happy!" She knows that's exactly what she loves about him, but it's also exactly the thing that makes making him face the music so much more difficult.

Seemingly sensing Sue's inner turmoil, Sheila begins to cry. David too, despite feeling that he maintained his position pretty well. Still, his insides tell him that all his reassurances are having no effect on Sue. Despite his pride, despite his hardheadedness, every instinct tells him to hug that woman. David wipes his nose with his elbow and wraps his arms around his wife. Sheila stops crying.

Figuring that she's finally got the bull's attention, Sue starts detailing the new plan of action, "I'm gonna hafta put Sheila in day care and find somethin' fast."

But a passive bull is still a bull and David's thick skull drops its jaw, "No kidda mine is gonna be raised by no

greasy child molester. You're her mother, you're stayin' home right here with our kid!" His holler, more of a knee-jerk reaction than an argument, falls to the floor without even an echo. Sue shakes her head sobbing. The pigeons flutter from the fence.

A humid patch of confined air lazily seeps into the failing wallpaper in the upper corner of Gale's bathroom. A flickering glow makes its way through the mist, dancing whimsically on the ceiling. Below, candles encircle Joe and Gale in an oversized bathtub, a damp CD player hosts new age music. Joe smiles with his eyes, "Thank you for a fantabulous meal."

"It was my pleasure," Gale smiles back.

"No, no. It was really somethin'." Joe's gaze doesn't break, "you, you're really somethin'. You know that?" He pauses; the suds pull his eyes away. "You deserve, you deserve …"

Gale boldly exposes his insecurity, "Somebody a lot better than you?"

"No…Just a guy a lot richer than me."

"Stop that." Gale leans forward slowly and plants a wet one on his pruned lips, "I got money – I want you." With that, her hands, like two stealthy sharks, suddenly grab his buns under the water. Joe jumps with the surprise of her advance. His face beaming with momentary joy, like that of a child. But as Gale closes her eyes to kiss again, his joy evaporates in the already moist air and eventually hides under the buckling wallpaper. By the time Gale's lips reach his, Joe's face has aged 30 years.

Day -13

Saturday morning, Eddie and Japeth, hand in hand, stroll down the local business strip. Eddie's got a thermos in his other hand, sipping coffee. The video game hangs out over the top of Japeth's back pocket.

"And then there's the new Atari, but it ain't what it use ta be. Bret 'n' Jimmy played that ages ago. It's like ancient." Japeth continues his steady stream of computer/game themed monologue.

"Ancient?" Eddie pops. That word somehow knocking him out of his half-listening glaze, "how old are you gonna be next week? Sixty?"

"Dad? Ten! The big One "O." Double digits!"

"That's right, you're a regular old man then. Aren't ya?"

Japeth has already moved on to other things. A large sign captures his attention. "Oh! Dad! This is it. The computer shop I was talkin' about."

Japeth tugs at his dad's hand while Eddie takes a deep breath as if to say, "This is not going to happen." But Japeth is already in the store and approaching the desktop PCs even before Eddie commences his sigh.

"This one's got a CD-RW/DVD combo drive," Japeth points and rolls the mouse, "woah check out that flat screen! And 512 meg!"

Japeth's excitement finally recedes enough for him to make eye contact with his father who is still standing at the door.

Countering Eddie's disinterest, Japeth speaks up, "And it's got Windows and a spreadsheet so you can do your account stuff on it too." Hoping that a little diplomacy might clinch the deal, "So everyone can use it!"

Eddie's focus is still out the door, when he sees something. Two short teenage boys run up the sidewalk. A bright red purse dangles from the shoulder of the kid on the left.

"Dad?" Japeth fishes.

Eddie steps out of the door just as the two teens pass. He times it just right so that the one with the purse steps directly into his sturdy body. Stopped by Eddie's robust chest, the boy falls to the ground back in the direction that he'd come from. The other boy flees from sight.

Looking down with narrowing eyes at the juvenile delinquent, Eddie steps on the strap securely and grumbles, "This purse don't match what yer wearin',"

The boy starts to get up, grabbing at the purse, but Eddie keeps his foot on the strap.

"Fuck you o' man!" the teen retorts. His bold verbiage obviously failing, the boy pulls a knife.

Eddie's narrowed eyes shift to disbelief. Not fear, but almost pure disgust. That fearless disgust slides right down Eddie's unbroken stare into the face of the young culprit causing consideration of yet another option. Turning the knife toward the purse, the boy relentlessly struggles to cut the strap. Eddie watches in nauseating amazement.

The computer shop owner steps out with a shotgun. The kid flees immediately. Eddie picks up the purse and walks back into the shop with the owner. They shake their heads.

"Damn kids," the shop owner quips.

Eddie grunts.

Japeth taps and clicks at one of the shop's best PCs, deeply engrossed in some bloody combat game. The blood-splattering graphics snap Eddie out of the purse incident.

"Japer! Come on!" Eddie commands, resounding with leftover disgust, "You know we ain't got that kinda money."

Without taking his eyes from the ghouls on screen, Japeth responds, "Are you sure? Did you check the purse?"

Shocked, Japeth's remark hits Eddie harder than a bolting teenage thief. Eddie ends his son's thought with a thunderous, "Japeth!"

Well aware of that tone, Japeth pauses the game and steps directly out of the store muttering to himself, "Geeze, I was only kidding…"

Eddie lets his son wait outside, puts the bright red purse up on the counter and pulls out an ID card. The shop owner hands him the phone.

Japeth walks up to the newspaper machine and stares at the headline: "Seven Alderman Caught in City Drug Sting."

"Kids today, I swear you can't trust any of 'em," the shop owner grumbles.

Eddie narrows his eyes at the shop owner and then through the window at Japeth outside. A crow lands ten feet from Japeth and fights off another for a piece of dried candy that had fallen from the purse.

All's quiet at David's house save for the sound of water splashing in the tub.

Baby Sheila, wide-eyed, and worried, "Mommy, Mommy."

David consoles, wiping her face with the sponge, "Mommy's takin' a break, babe. I think we're drivin' her crazy." David shrugs and spins a little toy boat bobbling on the water, "Okay, maybe it's me mostly drivin' her crazy." The little boat swirls as the infant pats the surface of the water with reddened hands.

Eddie and Japeth bob up and down inside Eddie's pickup. Japeth looks out the window at the row of identical posters stuck in the grass: "JJ Hayle for Mayor" and a picture

of JJ with that huge smile. Eddie doesn't notice. He's got the purse owner's ID up in his hands on the steering wheel, peeking down at it intently – as if to read the address, or perhaps, admire her photo. The Ohio State bird is stamped on the card, lending a peaceful dovelike presence to the woman's already attractive smile.

Back at the penthouse, JJ stands out on his terrace, the wind ruffling his slept-in pre-ruffled three piece suit (minus tie and jacket), the cloudy gray sky providing the only background. Chewing into the cell phone, smiling, smoking, JJ barks, "No shit? So how about the third race? Great, do it… Did you hear about Richardson? So you know what that means? Yeah … sure, do it."

JJ flips the phone closed. Dropping both hands on the railing, he looks over the city with a sigh. Maybe a thought, but not a worry. JJ never worries.

Down at ground level, a limo pulls up to his building. The current Mayor, Gerald Tyler, steps out as if triggering JJ's phone ringer. JJ once again pulls it out and flips it open, "Hayle … Yeah, I see him. Thanks." JJ shakes his head and chuckles at an apathetic bird perched a few feet down the railing.

Eddie's pickup rolls to a stop. The engine desperately tries to continue, coughing and spitting even after the ignition's been cut off. Eddie opens his door and eases out. After taking a second to look at the place, he turns back peering through his open window at Japeth playing with the video game, "Stay here."

Japeth nods without looking up. He's still feeling like Dad is upset with him. Eddie's in no hurry to relieve him of that burden.

A bit awkward with the red purse, Eddie climbs the front stairs, admiring the gorgeous cement pillars and

masonry work around the windows. He headnods "hello" to the gardner, who waves back with his chin. The house is huge and the entrance big enough that finding the bell takes a few extra moments. Eddie tucks his shirt in and presses the button. Chimes, not the fake electronic kind, but perhaps small church bells ring. In a second, a servant answers, tilts his head and raises an eyebrow.

Eddie speaks, "Uh," looking at the ID, "Is this the home of Kelly Gadar?"

"Gadeer... and yes." The servant sees the purse, knows the story. After looking Eddie over, correcting his pronunciation, and noticing Japeth in the truck, he finishes, "Right this way, sir."

Eddie enters the house impressed by the tasteful wooden furnishings and absolute spotlessness (especially compared to his home). Complementing the elegant home perfectly, a very good-looking woman in her mid-forties looks in from an adjoining room. She smiles while finishing up her phone conversation.

Eddie overhears the remains of that conversation, "That's what I said, all my credit cards. I was mortified, comatose..." The woman finishes a hearty laugh, "Charles, I'll call you back."

The servant smiles in her direction and backs out of the room.

"Well, thank you James," Kelly Gadeer turns her attentions to Eddie, "I recognize the purse, but I don't think we've met."

Eddie steps up nervously to shake her politely-extended hand, "Johnson, Eddie Johnson ... uhm ... I think you lost this."

Kelly accepts the purse, rummaging through it she smiles, "Lost? You really think I 'misplaced' it?"

Kelly opens the wallet fisting a wad of new Ben Franklins. She smiles playfully at Eddie and his lumberjack

physique, "You're too modest Mr. Johnson. I bet you spanked that little brat's ass."

Eddie's eyes widen at her crassness. She moves a bit closer to him, "Maybe I should spank yours ... show my appreciation."

Eddie looks down in embarrassment, "Well I.." Eddie's just about to say he's married, but notices the ring on her finger, "You're married!"

"Shit! That's right," Kelly dons a sexy smile, "Guess we'll just have to close the shutters."

"Uhm, look, my son's in the truck and I better get goin'."

Kelly changes gears, "Ah, I'm sorry. I mean, I only meant it as a compliment." She sighs. Opting for a more serious mood, she reaches again for her wallet, "If I can thank you in another way?"

"Thank you Miss, but I'm no ambulance chaser."

Kelly's chin backs into her neck. Feeling momentarily insulted, she watches Eddie make his way out of the huge house. He climbs into the truck. Kelly stands at the door and calls out without raising her voice, "If you change your mind…" And then under her breath, "You know where I live." She watches Eddie drive off, then fixes her lipstick in a dove-shaped mirror.

The moon takes its place in the sky. Its luminance falls through a window making waves of light and darkness across Gale's sea blue sheets. Gale and Joe, naked under those sheets, make the waves roll.

Day -12

The sun rolls out over JJ's lumberyard. Eddie, using an old pair of Henry's swimming goggles to shield his eyes,

pushes a huge plank across a table saw. Mounted under the table, the circular blade pokes its head above the plank like a shark fin splitting calm waters. The sound of metal chewing wood masks a conversation held by Joe and David just ten feet away. Putting the new forklift to good use, they shuffle lumber like cards. A limo pulls up. The driver rolls out of the front seat holding up a box of a dozen doughnuts and a brown bag, he shouts over the saw at JJ's kiosk, "I got the doughnuts and *cookies!*"

Larry, JJ's right-hand man, and the driver join JJ, already seated and watching the news in the kiosk.

Grabbing the bag, JJ tosses it in his safe and spins the combination knob, "Great! Let's make sure our cookies don't get stale."

Still smiling, eyes wide, he digs into the big box and falls backward into his worn rolling chair, "Didya get the o' fashioned? God, I love those o' fashioned!"

"Got dah old-fashioned, but dey're all outta dose sprinkly ones," the driver adds.

"'at's okay, I'll live," JJ snorts as the three grown men pig out on pastries.

Eddie grabs another plank and continues. David leverages a crate of wood with the lift. Joe watches as the three suited men close the box of doughnuts, lock the office/kiosk, slip into the limo and drive off. Jumping on the forklift as David passes, Joe yells into David's ear, "You like Doughnuts?"

"What?" David yells back.

"Look, JJ just dumped a shitloada dirty money in that fuckin' safe of his ... Wouldn't it be nice to have some extra cash?"

David cuts the motor on the lift, "Are you serious?"

"Come on man, you were just tellin' us about yer problems with Sue. I mean, yer house is gonna look a little bare without that 27-inch."

"Jesus, Joe, I don't know."

"It's not like it's wrong. I mean it's fuckin' JJ's dirty money. It ain't even nobody's."

"Yeah, but he'd kill us. I mean really kill us. As in dead," David bites his lip, "then Sue'd really be pissed at me."

"Davey, Davey. I've been watchin' these guys. They ain't playin' jacks. They're moving serious money around. Serious, like you don't come back here tomorrow. Serious, like you're set for a fuckin' year in some other town."

"You sure there's that kinda money in there?"

"You know all that crap Tyler's in. Ain't you been reading the paper?" Joe yanks last weeks news from under David's butt and whacks him in the head with it, "I'm bettin' JJ's got a price on his head too. We'd be the least of his problems."

"Even if that's true -- he ain't dead yet. What if he catches us before we get that safe open?"

"He's in a fucking limo! You think you can see that thing comin'? Now go hit up Eddie for the keys to the fucking office."

David climbs out of the lift while looking Joe in the eyes to make sure he's on the level. He steps up to Eddie who is at the table saw whistling, so deeply engrossed in his work that he doesn't even notice David. David stands for about ten seconds and then yells over the saw, "Keys!"

Eddie continues without reaction, but now he's ignoring David instead of just being oblivious. He finishes the cut, then pulls the silly goggles up to his forehead before taking a deep sigh, "What?"

Saw still scraping, David mouths the word 'keys" as he points toward the keys on the ring plugged into the saw power switch.

Eddie flips the saw off, "Whadjya want the keys for?"

The saw winds down. David is a bit nervous by now, "JJ and the guys, they ahh, left some doughnuts in the office. Joe and I, we're dying for a jelly-filled about now."

Eddie, looking over David's shoulder, sees Joe scamming the office. Eddie grabs another plank readies it for the cut and says to David, "What do you really want the keys for?"

Several blocks away from the yard, a phone rings in the limo. The driver answers.

"God I love dose sprinkly things though," JJ chuckles over a mouthful.

Larry nods in pseudo-amusement. The driver pulls over and turns to the two in the back, "Dat was Tyler, he wants dah limo back."

"Jesus doesn't he know he's almost last weeks' news?" JJ whines.

"Yeah, but this week," Larry reminds, "it's still his limo."

The driver apologizes, "Sorry JJ, I'll drop yous two at dah rental place."

Back at the yard, David whispers to Eddie, "Look Eddie, Joe thinks JJ's got some major bucks in the safe … I mean it's just dirty money anyways."

Eddie answers by turning his head and switching the saw back on. Joe, suspecting this hiccup in his little plan, steps up assertively and reaches for the keys. Eddie grabs Joe's hand and stares him down like the kid on the street with the red purse.

Joe yelling clearly over the saw, "Jesus fucking Christ, Eddie! Haven't you had enough of this shit?"

At the nearby rental place, Larry's hand turns the key, starting up a tan Ford Escort.

"You know what Larry?" JJ slides in.

"No. What?" Larry answers blankly.

"I want another friggin' doughnut."

At the yard, Joe pulls his arm away from Eddie, all the while keeping an eye on those keys in the saw. Fervent, Joe is showing no sign of changing his mind, "Just give me the fuckin' keys!"

Eddie stops sawing and stands arms-folded directly between Joe and the keys. Joe eyes Eddie with frustration and resolve, he grabs a handy crowbar off the lift and restates his demands. Eddie isn't budging. David's jaw drops.

The tan Ford pulls up to the yard gate. JJ peers out the window, "Wait, wait. Park out here."

Larry pulls over, rolls down his window, folds his arms like Eddie and watches the three workmen settle their dispute.

Joe's head is shaking back and forth, "Come on Eddie, don't make me do this."

David takes a few steps away. Eddie pulls the keys from the machine and drops them down the sewer grate. Joe drops to the ground in a pathetic attempt to save them. "Jesus Christ, David! Go get the damn forklift, we'll ram that fuckin' office open."

David hesitantly starts the lift and slowly heads toward the office. Joe gets up quickly, rage pouring out of his eyes like blood, he backhands the crowbar across Eddie's face. Eddie doubles over, hands to his head. Stars spark through the darkness from one ear to the other.

Joe walks over to the office, "Right here, ram it right here."

"What about Eddie?" David worries.

"Shut up, he got what he deserved. Ram the fuckin' thing!"

David aims, hits the gas and plows a hole into JJ's office as JJ and Larry watch in an amused kind of surprise.

JJ shakes his head, "What kinda jerk'd take a crowbar to dah head? And for what? To save an asshole like me a coupla bucks?"

"Not me," Larry confirms, "You can bet on it."

"My point exactly. My point exactly. My whole goddamned life, nobody, *nobody*, done somethin' dat dumb for me. Not a one."

"Relax JJ. We can get more money outta the insurance for dah office wreck, than you had in dah fuckin' safe."

"Yeah Lar, you too, yer a goddamn leech. You got one hand in my pocket rattlin' my nuts." JJ glosses over in a very rare moment of reflection, "Not a one. But this fuckin' Eddie Johnson. This fuckin' Eddie Johnson -- what the hell is he thinkin'? A crowbar to dah skull, for a shit like me?"

Larry shakes his head and takes a breath at JJ getting all 'moved.' They both pause to marvel at Joe and Davie as they mash the kiosk office with the new forklift.

Larry ends the pause, "Sure as shit, beats the hell outta me."

JJ's introspection gives way to laughter, "Larry put this guy in my fuckin' will -- give him the goddamn yard when I go."

Larry rolls his eyes, "I'll make a note of it."

JJ chuckles, "At least I'll do one friggin' decent thing right."

Larry raises an eyebrow, "Yeah, but you'll be dead before you know it."

"Call a goddamn ambulance for the bonehead." Gradually narrowing eyes contrast JJ's grin, as Larry's last comment starts to sink in, "…what's that s'posed to mean?"

David and Joe are already in the office with JJ's newest piece of machinery, tearing up the place. They

skewer the safe with the forklift and wheel it over to Joe's truck, dumping it in the back. Both silently serious, hearts pumping and determined, they hop in and start to peel out. But Larry has the Ford Escort blocking the gates and JJ is out in front of the rental car with his cigarette lit and pistol drawn right at Joe's side of the windshield. Davie is terrified, while JJ's pleased as a pig in shit to have caught them so red-handed. He's going to enjoy his little *Serpico* moment.

Joe grunts, red-eyed, punches the throttle up within twenty feet of the Al Pacino wannabe before skidding the truck to a stop.

"Dis ain't no candy shop, Mr. Stacey." JJ pigeon puffs his chest, "it's big business." Though he has no intention of using it, JJ engages the pistol to accentuate his speech.

Davie's jaw is still down, he stupidly puts his hands up and freezes. Joe shakes his head and fists the steering wheel. St. Joseph falls off the dash with the whack. Sirens can be heard in the distance.

Larry leans his head out the window toward JJ and clears his throat, "Ahheem, JJ Hayle guns down two in cold blood. Not the most desirable headline -- aye? *Mayor?"*

If Eddie were conscious he could have looked up for that precious little moment to have seen JJ with his cold black pistol waving, chest out, tie loosened, grin sparkling, standing directly in front of a huge "JJ for Mayor" billboard across the street. JJ's current smile echoing that same golden Scarface grin printed at one thousand times actual size just a matter of fifty feet behind him.

JJ shrugs his shoulders and rolls his head. "Yup! Good point." He holsters the gun then, shouting over to Joe, "Alright, Alright yous two. Get dat box offa dat truck and get outta here. By dah way, yer both fired."

Joe hops out of the truck, slaps the bed gate open, walks back into the cab casting his steely eyes at JJ. He

slams the door, punches the accelerator -- the safe tumbles off the bed and onto the ground. Joe slams the break, bringing his truck to within a few feet of JJ and his grin. JJ's hands are out to either side like a matador. His shoulders pitch upward and he chuckles. Reveling in the drama, JJ struts to the right. Larry backs the Escort as JJ, almost in a bow, waves his arm, palm up, allowing Joe and Davie to pass and never return. JJ's smile happily fills his face.

Joe peels off. JJ grabs his belly as he belts out a few uncontrollable ho-ho-ho's of laughter.

Larry shakes his head, "Yer a real jolly fuckin' Santa Clause, ain't ya?"

A squad car and ambulance roll into the lot. JJ, still bent over laughing, points his finger in the direction of Eddie. The paramedics rush over. The cops look up at JJ with a "What do you want us to do here?" expression. JJ shakes his head and waves them off.

Larry hovers over the paramedics as they tend to Eddie. JJ finally takes a breath and gives his smile a break. He sits down in the half-demolished office, flips on the TV and grabs a doughnut. The paramedics strap an incoherent Eddie up on the stretcher then carry him to the ambulance.

Yelling through the doughnut at Eddie, "I'm closin' the yard fer a week. I want you back here next Monday, Johnson. Get me two new men." JJ swallows, "how 'bout dat kid a yers?"

Eddie, of course, doesn't respond to JJ, half conscious, a face full of blood, Eddie struggles to make sense of these men in white, tubes and bandages strapped around him, and the sterile vehicle. "Emily? Emily?"

The sirens once again spark up, scaring a single pigeon into flight. Flying above the city, the pigeon watches the emergency lights get smaller and smaller. It hovers higher and higher until the twirling lights from other emergency vehicles, busy with various other problems in

various other parts of the city, prick little bleeding pin holes in his view -- little bubbling red lights, like bullet holes in a dead man.

Not one of the eight fog lights on the rack atop Joe's pickup shines as the truck pulls up to David's house. David steps tentatively out. He stops just before closing the door and almost breaks the punishing silence of the ride with a word, a question, something. David's mouth opens, then pauses, given Joe's blank eyes, dull as the fog lights, they aren't extending any kind of invitation for conversation. David closes his mouth and the door. Joe pulls promptly away. David stands dumbfounded, fighting off that all too familiar feeling that things are going to quickly get even worse.

"David!" He hears his name in Sue's pissed off voice. She has a way of making the "V" scrape his inner ear like the edge of a chipped chisel. Squeezing his eye shut and preparing for a punch in the face, he turns toward his house.

Sue, with Sheila in arms stands in a failing attempt to look tough. Two men in blue jump suits carry his 27 inch television set to a white van.

David's brain finally sparks out of the confusion, "Shit! Repo-men! Oh Babe, Babe, I'm sorry. I'm so sorry."

Sue's rage dissolves into depletion, on the edge of tears, "What are you doing here? It's not even 4 o'clock?

David turns his red eyes to the ground, "I'm sorry."

"Jesus, David, you lost this job too! David!!!" Sue's anticipated tears dissipate as disgust takes over her lips. First stepping slowly, then at a brisk clip, she canters over to the repo-van. "The least you guy's could do is give me a ride to the west side."

Taking a look at the broken David, the repo-men check each other and nod a 'why not?'. David stands impotent as the van drives off. His head still down, arms

close at his sides, he keeps his face away from the van, but stretches his view to watch Sue with the baby. He doesn't turn enough to see her mouth the words "I love you" through the van window.

Straight face holding back a storm, Joe gathers his things from Gale's home. A picture of the two of them smiling, taped to the mirror, stops his stride. With only the smallest of facial muscle movements he casts a reflection of shame at himself, pulls out a pen and note paper from the top drawer. He almost starts to write something, then tosses the paper and pen clumsily into the drawer, slamming it shut all in one motion as he turns for the door.

Eddie's three boys sit, long faced and silent, in the hospital waiting room. Sam writes a letter to his girlfriend as Henry finishes a prayer and casts an angry eye at Japeth playing on the pocket video game.

Henry shames, "How could you play games? This is your father! Show some respect."

Japeth sniffles and wipes his nose. Without looking at Henry, he quietly shuts off the game and puts his head down.

Sam whispers to Henry, "Take it easy, dude. There's nothing he can do. Let him play."

Standing in his light tan trench coat, his back to the boys, Larry faces the window reading the paper. The headline: "Driveby Shooting Spree."

Finally, the surgeon steps in removing his mask. He's a magnet for swollen eyes.

"You the Johnson boys?" The doctor sighs.

Henry stands up, "Yes, sir."

The doctor looks over at Larry, "And you?"

Larry, looking like JJ made him be there, apathetically grunts, "Friend a dah family."

Sam can't wait through the formalities, "Is he alive?"

The doctor cracks a smile, "He's alive. He's fine... but he's ... lost an eye."

Japeth, who hasn't moved since Henry scolded him, sniffles again and wipes his nose. A tear drops on the floor between his dangling legs.

JJ shuffles around his apartment, still in the same suit, still on the cell phone. The TV's not been shut off for a week. He checks on a frozen pizza bubbling in the oven and burns his finger.

"Shit!" JJ puts his finger in his mouth to soothe the pain, "No, no not you, the damn oven... anyway, his right eye? Huh, damn. Ya think he's a lefty? Ha!"

JJ chuckles and licks his finger and says, "Yeah, Yeah ... look take his kids out for some ... ah, burgers ... kids like burgers, right? Uh-huh. Uh-huh. Just do it, Lar! You know, buy 'em some friggin' french fries."

Larry bites down into a quarter pound hamburger at the local kid-oriented fast food place, not even trying to hide the "I'd rather be someplace else" look on his face. The boys, who usually love the restaurant, chew slowly and somberly. Japeth isn't eating at all. Instead, he maintains the same seated looking-down position.

"Look kid," Larry is bored into showing some compassion. "It's just an eye. He's got another one."

Sam answers, "It's his birthday."

Larry pauses mid-chomp, "Who? Eddie's?" He asks in a food-muffled breath.

"No his!" Sam points at Japeth.

Larry, still holding the burger up to his mouth, swings his slightly amused eyes to little Japeth sulking at the other end of the table. "That's kind of a sucky thing to uhm, happen on your birtday. Yeah, sorry about dat, kid."

Henry interjects pointedly, "He's used to it."

Though Larry missed the reference, Sam knows the cheap shot Henry's just taken. Pointing his elbow in kind, Sam jabs Henry in the ribs (a dangerous move, Sam being the smaller of the two). Henry ignores the jab.

"What ah, whaddaya want? I mean, What was yer dad gonna buy ya? For yer birtday?"

Japeth looks up for the first time, "A computer!" he proclaims surprisingly loudly, almost as a jab back at Henry.

Larry's eyes widen, "A computer?"

"An accelerated chip with at least two gigahertz and 500 megs of video memory." Japeth expands with an unexpected inflection of determined frustration.

Day -5

A week later, JJ, with a rolled up newspaper under his arm, checks out the rebuilt office kiosk. He's amused for mere seconds; he grunts, then sits down on the old chair, tosses his feet up and pages through the news. The headline: "Body Parts For Sale, City Morgue Under Investigation." Eddie steps into the office, a black patch over his right eye. Heading straight to the time clock, Eddie punches his card.

JJ watches him the whole time, grinning, waiting for an "hello," a headnod ... something from the headstrong Eddie.

JJ can no longer bear the wait, "What? That's it? You take a crowbar to dah head, an eyeball later, yer back to work as usual? Like nothin' happened?

Eddie stops, turns his face toward JJ, but says nothing.

"You're somethin' Johnson," JJ laughs, "Really somethin'."

"Thanks for treating my kids," Eddie finally replies, "I appreciate that."

JJ fakes a serious expression, "Now don't get all gushy on me," mocking Eddie, "'Thanks for treatin' my kids?' Yer breakin' what little heart I got left."

Eddie's just lost an eye. JJ's ribbing makes no dents.

JJ reaches into his briefcase. "Brace yerself Eddie, JJ Hayle is about to thank *you!*" JJ clears his throat to be dramatic, "It's come to my attention dat yer family is short one computer."

Proudly JJ flips open the briefcase revealing a laptop. He sets it up on the desk. Eddie stands mute.

"Look at dis, top a dah line, built in modem, you can see dah status a dah fuckin' Wall Street stocks anytime you want, and check dis out, you can watch a full feature movie on these fuckin' little disks -- right here on dah computer!"

Eddie smiles modestly, his eye a bit red. "That's nice, real nice, but I couldn't..."

JJ, disappointed, interrupts, "Fuck you Eddie! It ain't for you," he waves his cigarette for punctuation. "It's for dat little one ah yers. Jamie or Jagged or..."

"Japeth." Eddie corrects.

"What kind a crappy name is dat?" JJ barks, "Anyway, while you're out gettin' your forehead bashed in ... Jangle is havin' a birtday."

Eddie exhales a long breath. Such a long breath, it's as if he's held it even before the knock on the head, "You're right. Japeth will really like this. Thank you."

Eddie puts the timecard back into his pocket and walks off to work, it's obvious that accepting charity is not a skill that comes comfortably to him. JJ shakes his head at Eddie, then chuckles to himself, "No. No. Thank *you!*"

Eddie returns to his truck rummaging for some tools, JJ hangs out of the office door, "Hey Johnson, I need a couple a more guys around here. Get me some."

Eddie and Henry stand in front of the kitchen sink cleaning off plates from a rather mediocre dinner. Eddie focuses his one eyeball down into the suds, but his mind is someplace else. He doesn't notice Henry studying the eye-patch. He can't see the frustration and anger that simply won't be expressed simmering inside Henry. Though fitted with two good eyes, ironically, Henry blinds himself to Eddie's silent, fatherly love.

In the front room Japeth sits near an open briefcase; he's set up JJ's computer and has his nose buried in the manuals. Sam watches the news: "Still no relief for farmers as their pocket books dry up with the weather..."

"That error again!" Japeth grumbles over to Sam, "The same one. Inaccessible address or whatever."

"Try shutting it off and turning it on again." Sam replies blankly, not interested in the news, but seemingly unable to turn his head away from the TV.

By now Henry's starving stare has shifted to a photo of a younger Johnson family hanging next to the window. The photo pre-dates Japeth, but was taken prior to Mrs. Johnson's untimely death. She's smiling and pregnant, Henry's smiling, Eddie and Sam are grinning as well.

"It wasn't his fault, Henry." Eddie speaks, jarring a far-away Henry out of his nostalgia.

Henry wasn't expecting his father to take note, certainly not respond -- dead on, no less. Henry tosses the last dish on the tray and runs out. Eddie takes a deep breath and leans his head, heavy with thoughts, against the cupboard above the sink. He sneezes suddenly, catching all that dirty snot and sawdust in his big hands.

Smoke and overweight men in sloppy suits fill Mayor Tyler's living room. JJ enjoys a drink among them. The conversations ramble from politics to marital problems.

"Richardson was it. Now they've got us by the balls." An alderman brings up the most pressing issue.

"Got *you* by the balls," Tyler corrects.

"Tyler," JJ smiles, "Give it up big guy. It's a bad situation, but it doesn't hafta take dah whole fuckin' party outta office."

Tyler, too angry to look at JJ (or too disgusted), hyperventilates, "No, not the party, just me!"

A lawyer chimes in, "We've been over this. Bob's already agreed."

Tyler pulls his tie off. A respectful silence turns awkward.

"Jesus," JJ breaks the silence, "Did you see that body part shit in the paper?"

The alderman lightens up, relieved to change the topic. "Yeah, you wanna buy a fucking kidney, just go down to the morgue."

Tyler's eyes narrow, "It's probably fucking Richardson's kidney."

JJ breaks out into laughter. Tyler finally directs his eyes at JJ -- they're not amused.

Day -4

All is quiet at David's home, save for his snoring. A honk from outside wakes him. Groggy and fearing the worst, he shuffles over to the window -- cautiously peeking out. In the street, Eddie, in his truck, headnods David to come on out.

David jumps in surprise, bumping his head on the top of the window. Dressing quickly, an alarmed David yells out the window, "Jesus, Eddie! I didn't know he hit you. I mean, I didn't know he was gonna hit you!" David eyes the back door, "Shit.... Just don't hurt me. It was Joe. Joe all the way."

"I know it was Joe," Eddie yells toward the window, "I need some help at the yard."

David halts his rush to escape. He calms down, gathers a few things and steps out sheepishly. "You're not mad at me?"

"I need another set a hands at the yard."

"But JJ? JJ'll kill me."

"JJ told me to hire a couple a guys. I'm hiring you."

David looks down in shame, "Thank you Eddie, thank you."

Eddie takes a peek around the house, "Sue? Sheila?"

"She took off to her mom's last week. I haven't seen her since. I'm rotting. I'm just rottin' here, Eddie."

"Jesus, stop that talk and get in."

Eddie and David pull up to the empty yard. Only a little surprised not to see JJ, Eddie opens the new office and the two stamp their cards. David, as silent as a scolded Japeth, scans the office uncomfortably. An ashtray, a stack of newspapers, a quiet TV set.

Eddie finishes the stamping and grunts, "All right."

David notices JJ's cell phone opened under a magazine.

A phone rings in Joe's girlfriend's place. A silent answering machine adjacent to her round bed perks up, "Hi, this is Gale Jefferies, I'm not in, just leave a message ... Joe, I miss you." **Beep**.

After a moment of silence, **click**, the caller hangs up. A pigeon takes flight from Gale's window. It flies high over the city, coming to rest on JJ's billboard across from the yard. A limo pulls up in front. Larry takes his time getting out; a paper rolled up under his arm. He smirks at the sight of David working alongside Eddie. Eddie takes no notice. Larry continues his step into the office, drops the newspaper on top

of the time clock, the headline: "JJ Hayle Found Dead in Street." The accompanying photo captures a black and white JJ in 'that same suit' lying twisted in a pool of black blood curbside.

With a 'shit happens' sigh, Larry steps to the sink, splashes his face, rinses his hands, waving them dry on the way back to the limo.

Eddie's truck bumps down poor pavement. Dirt from the dry road powders up into the dark evening sky. Eddie flips the radio on: "...And up in the mid 80's. Looks like we have some cloud cover for the first time since May. I want to predict rain, but I've been wrong too many times this summer. So let's just hope for it..."

Click! Eddie flips the radio off and parks in the nearly empty lot of a dismal funeral home. The director leads him to the room, then leaves Eddie alone with the dearly departed. Eddie slowly steps up to the casket and squints his eye. JJ lies dead as a doornail, a peaceful, yet shit-eating grin relaxed on his lifeless face.

"Paaaahhhh," Eddie sighs and starts to turn, but is surprised to see two silhouetted trench-coated men standing behind him.

"Oh, I'm sorry." Eddie apologizes.

"No, we're not here for him." One of the men corrects, " He's dead. We're here for *you*."

"Me?"

The one man then steps into the light; it's Larry, "Hey Eddie."

"Hey," Eddie responds for lack of a better word.

Larry smiles at Eddie's naiveté, "Yeah, JJ, well, he was a mother-fucker. I'm sure you'd agree. But dat day,

Eddie, he had dis stroke a 'goodness', 'inspiration' if you will. Basically, he left you dah lumberyard." Larry slaps some documents onto Eddie's big chest, "Here's dah deed, sign it and bada boom bada bing ... it's yers."

"I don't get it?"

"You get it!" Larry looks at his associate with an amused grin, "Jesus Christ, dis guy's looking at me with one fuckin' eye and he still doesn't have dah damnedest clue." Larry shakes his head back at Eddie, "You stood up for him for no good reason Eddie. You 'inspired' him to do one decent thing and you know what? Me too. I coulda just as easily left ya out of dat fuckin' will. JJ probably didn't even expect me ta keep ya in. But I was there when dey cracked ya open, Eddie. Any guy takes a crack like dat deserves the friggin' sawdust bin. It's yers man ... God bless ... or whatever."

Eddie pulls the deed off his chest. Larry headnods and exits with the associate. Giving one last look at JJ, Eddie picks some wood chips out of his eyebrow and shuffles slowly out into the parking lot. Larry's limo is just pulling away, its headlights illuminating the gravestones. Eddie stuffs the deed in his pocket, pulls out his picture of Emily and looks up into the dark cloudy heavens.

Puffy white clouds track across the color LCD screen of Japeth's new computer, he and Sam try out screen-saver designs back at the Johnson residence. Henry is on the recliner reading the Bible. Eddie, late for dinner, takes his plate out of the fridge and eats quietly standing over the sink. A rare silence rafts through the rooms of the Johnson home.

Day -2

Under cloudy, but bright skies, David shows Henry how to operate the forklift. Eddie takes a breather from the table saw to watch David and his son. By now the two are goofing off a bit. David has a rope, he's riding the forklift like a cowboy and swinging the lasso trying to nab Henry who's indulging in a smile. They're both laughing. Eddie watches the two peacefully, smiling inside, he fades into a memory of a young small Johnson family. In his mind's eye, a toddling two-year-old Henry struggles to control a gushing garden hose, watering down a laughing long-haired Emily.

Waking from a troubled sleep, Eddie wraps himself in the flannel robe Emily had bought him one Father's Day. He sniffs the cloth's scent while checking on each of his sleeping children. Lingering at Henry's door, Eddie silently stares at his first born son, who peacefully snores. Eddie sighs himself into another nostalgic memory and then whispers, "Why can't you and me get along this well when we're both awake?"

Retiring to the darkened living room, Eddie flips on the laptop. The light from the LCD screen reflects off his rugged face. He takes a deep breath and cracks open some software manuals. Glancing up at the clock, Eddie's surprised to see most of the night is gone. A scratch to the beard, another look back at the manual, he plops a few numbers into the spreadsheet cells and hits enter. The result is negative, a tired Eddie drops his head into his big hands. He repeats the procedure -- still negative.

Day 0

"Where's Henry!" Eddie looks around his recently inherited lumberyard.

David, surprised by such volume from Eddie, stutters to answer, "He said, some, something about a Bible study or somethin'."

"We only get him a coupla hours a day. Jesus, we need him today!"

Surprised to hear Eddie complain, David stands silent.

"Great!" Eddie snarls sarcastically, "me and you here an extra hour then."

"Okay, Eddie, no problem. I'll get the lift over."

The two workers start up the forklift. They capture a large crate, but the lift won't engage. They try, but the machine only whines.

"It's jammed, " David shrugs, "A brand new machine and it's jammed."

"Maybe you shouldn't go ramming it into walls."

David goes stone cold quiet.

"Christ! Don't just stand there!" Eddie commands, "Go get the damn tool set."

David stumbles off immediately and returns hesitantly with the tool set. The two get down on their hands and knees. They work on the machine for nearly two hours.

"Try it now." Eddie directs.

David pulls the lever, but the machine only whines, now louder than before.

"Hand me the crowbar." Eddie says calmly.

David looks over at Eddie as if Eddie were an erect grizzly drooling all over himself. He sheepishly picks up the crowbar and reluctantly hands it over to Eddie. Eddie grabs it hard, turns toward the machine and, with all his might,

recklessly whacks the forklift. Over and over, he whacks the forklift.

David gasps, then leaps onto Eddie's back, "Eddie! Eddie! Relax! Take it easy!"

Eddie, with David on his back, leans belly over the forklift engine. He squeezes his eye hard, but does not cry. The two lay there for a full minute, Eddie's breaths causing David to bob slightly up and down.

Henry drops back on his bed, Bible in hand. Five other teens his age sit around his room, a few on the floor. One on the chair reads, "...If you were blind, you would not have any sin. But now that you insist 'We see,' your sin remains..."

Eddie and David drive out of the yard. The truck digs into the dirt smack in front of that huge billboard and JJ's ironic smile.

"So ah,... Sue?" Eddie asks David, trying to show he's doing better.

"Naw, she ain't back yet. I mean, I really messed up this time. Pretty good this time. I wouldn'ta had a prayer, 'cept that you showed up." David buttons his lips for a second. "I heard from her mother that she was impressed. I mean, if *you* think I'm worth comin' back to, Eddie, well you know."

The two pull up to David's empty house and Eddie drops David off. A few turns and a couple of city stoplights later, Eddie comes to a stop at the highway on-ramp. Slam! A squeegee splats down on the windshield. Eddie jerks back in surprise. The jarring clunk splashes water on the dry glass still displaying smears from last week's cabbage patch man. Eddie snaps out of his alarm and looks for the old man. Instead, a punk kid slaps a begging hand up to the window as if to say...'out with the bucks dude!'

Eddie narrows his eyes, "Where's the old man?"

"Fuck the old man. Where's my five spot?" the kid pops back without a thought.

The lights change, Eddie confounded, still looking around for the old man, takes the opportunity to drive off. The kid yells some obscenity and tosses the squeegee at the truck in anger. It hits the back window and falls into the bed.

In front of the Johnson home, Japeth watches his friend Jimmy totter atop a pair of homemade stilts.

"This is so cool," Jimmy wobbles. "Your dad made these?"

"Yeah." Japeth answers, "He was gonna giv'em to me for my birthday, but then his boss, that JJ Hayle guy, he gave me the laptop, so Pops gave these to Sam."

"That's how he lost his eye? Somethin' with that JJ guy?"

Jimmy takes a couple more uncertain steps and falls. Eddie pulls up.

"Hey Dad!" Japeth welcomes.

Eddie looks past him, "Where's your brothers?"

"Henry's in his room with his Bible heads. Sam called. There's a message on the machine, he's takin' Jeanie out to dinner or somethin'. It's Henry's night, but I don't think he's gonna cook. So...."

"So?"

"So what's for dinner? And is it okay if Jimmy eats over?"

Eddie grunts and walks into the house with no more of an answer than that. The house is a bit of a mess, the TV left blaring: "... the identical twin who plotted to kill her twin sister. We'll be right back with the real life court room drama..."

Eddie hooks the TV set cord on his foot and with one kick pulls the plug out of the wall. **Click.**

He then peeks into Henry's room. He can hear one of Henry's friends as he approaches, "...Paul says in Corinthians that we've got to ..."

Eddie charges into the room without hiding his mood. "Did Paul tell you not to make dinner!"

The teens look up silent and shocked.

"You agreed to make dinner tonight. If you were unable to make arrangements otherwise, then you oughta be makin' dinner right now." Eddie points with his poking eye at his son. "A man's word is his honor!"

"But dad, I, I also promised these guys I'd do the Bible study here tonight. Is it really such a big deal? Sam trades with me all the time."

"Sam's not gonna be here for dinner." Eddie looks over the silent group of kids in concession, but not approval. "Forget it, I'll make dinner!" Grumbling as he leaves, "A man's word!"

Down in the kitchen, Eddie opens the fridge, then the freezer, and then the cupboards. A few cans of ravioli and a box of macaroni and cheese. He looks up at Emily, splashes his face with water and then looks in the mirror. A very uncommon spirit of exhaustion leaks from him like air from the brakes of a train as Eddie Johnson indulges in a private moment of despair. He squeezes his eye and starts to whimper to himself. Lifting his patch, he rubs his big dirty hands across the tears. Distracted with his current condition he doesn't hear the floorboard-muffled voices of Henry and friends discussing the virtues of helping people in need.

"Emily! Emily!" Eddie cries out in need.

Henry and friends reciprocate by not hearing him.

"She musta been one hell of a woman."

Eddie turns in surprise. The voice is not that of a child. Eddie's eyes widen to see JJ reaching in the fridge, blood staining his two piece suit.

JJ, still with his face in the fridge, "Yeah, I seen you pullin' out dat ratty photo of her two or tree times a day." JJ slides a gallon of milk to the side, the refrigerator light reflecting off his squinting eyes, "Man, I'm fuckin' parched. Don't you got even a one goddamn beer?"

Moments earlier Eddie's eye sockets were mere slits, squeezing out the tears. Now they're frozen open, the good one, the bad one -- both in dried sweat, tears, with sawdust rounding. Eddie brings his forearm up to his face in an attempt to rub away the mess there that's surely creating this illusion or hallucination. But, the rubbing fails to wipe away JJ. "I watched 'em bury you!" Eddie finally mutters.

"Yeah, dat was sweet. Yer a goddamn teddy bear. First you give an eye to me, then you show up for my funeral. Dey musta knocked any sense outta ya with dat crowbar." With his head still in the icebox, JJ pushes over a spoiling jar of mayo. "Not even a fuckin' Cola?"

"You're dead JJ. Twelve bullets to the chest."

"Shame on you Eddie, that sounds like a newspaper headline. Didn't you give that up for Lent or somethin'?"

"I didn't give up anything for Lent, that's my son. I don't go for that religious stuff."

"Oh yeah? That ain't what God says," JJ takes a swig of some sugary fruit juice," Yer right about one thing Eddie. I'm a dead man. Dead as a fuckin' doornail. And you know about the dead ... dey go up or dey go down. I'm so friggin flabbergasted dat I went up!" JJ dramatically points up at the ceiling. "Man can you believe dat?" He chuckles to himself, "I was one serious bastard. I couldn't give a rat's ass 'bout nobody but JJ Hayle. But you... Eddie fuckin' Johnson, takin' a crowbar to dah head, yer little eyeball splattering like a goddamn chicken egg. Wheww, now dat, dat was really somethin'."

JJ shuts up for a second, pats his own heart in sincerity, chuckles one more time, then takes another swig

while checking his shirt pockets, "You gotta cigarette? God I'm dying for a smoke. Hah! dyin'! Anyway, your little eye-smashin' event, that hit me. Never felt nothin' like dat before. And I've seen a lot worse -- guys gettin' killed and shit. Christ, I didn't even feel anythin' when I got dat lead in my ribs. All dat lead. But you standin' up for me. If I knew how to cry - I woulda."

Eddie closes his eyes for a long time, lifts his patch (as if the missing eye could do a better job) and takes just one more hopeful gaze.

"Yeah, I kinda thought you'd have a problem with dis," JJ rolls his eyes over his own virtual reincarnation, "me here and all. Anyway, dah top banana, he's an even stiffer Joe than you, he sent me down. Some kinda poetic justice or somethin'. Guess he figured you'd have even a bigger problem if it was him drinkin' your kids' fuckin' fruit juice insteada me."

"Top banana?"

"Yeah, you know. The big guy. Head honcho. The man upstaris -- all that shit. Come on, bonehead -- God! God sent me here. I'm a dead man! Wise up! You need another whack in dah skull?"

Eddie's eye still bulging, his head shaking, "God? I don't go tah church. I don't even read the Bible. I'm not into that. That's my son, Henry. I'm a lumberyard foreman."

JJ sighs, shakes his head back at Eddie and then morphs into Emily. Eddie immediately grabs his heart and falls to one knee. Emily smiles, peaceful and sympathetic, then morphs into all the people Eddie has ever known to die, finally ending up back as JJ. But now JJ's voice is different, much softer, gentler, older, "Edward, I am sad too. Like you, I've worked hard to create a good life. I have exhausted my heart for my children. I am married to my work, but my work has been unfaithful. Like yours, my wife has died giving birth."

Far too much for Eddie, these words bring him to both knees and one hand on the floor -- simply bellowing, "But I, but, I'm not a religious man. I don't even go tah church."

JJ's mouth with the gentler voice continues, "But you praise me because you worship my work. I watch you, Edward Johnson, delighting in the simple task of living. No one sees it in you, but I do. Quietly, at work and at home, you are happy. You respect me because you respect yourself. You love me because you love the life that I have given you. Your allegiance to me is sadly so very obvious in the way you treat my children."

Eddie slobbers, mucus from his nose, tears from his eyes, drool to the floor, "Sadly so obvious?"

"I'd prefer that your personal care not stand out. That means it's solitary. So very sadly solitary. You are honorable Edward. Honorable. How many other honorable people do you know? Do you know even one? Honesty has died; my children have died. Edward, you are a better father than I."

Eddie's head rocks back and forth uncontrollably, "Oh, my God. Oh, my God."

"I'm afraid it has come to the point ...well, yes, to the point of tears. There was a time when all was good, and then I watched it sour and then, again, I started over. I'm only doing my best. Just like you. But I'm growing so tired of watching my youngest children mistreated, hurt and ultimately killed on the inside. I'm afraid it's reached the point of tears again. You haven't been reading the papers. You are the only one left Edward Johnson. You are the only one still alive I trust to love."

"I don't even go tah church -- what about Henry?" Eddie pleads.

"Henry is a confused young man. Perhaps he'll stumble across my path. But what he's really seeking is a

reason for his mother's death. That, and relief from the guilt he feels for blaming Japeth for that death."

Eddie returns to his slobbering.

"Oh Edward," the JJ/God continues, "everyone is searching for something to satisfy their own insecurities. They aren't looking out for each other. Just stumbling around longing for direction instead of love. So anyway, it's a runaway train. I need a sand embankment. I need a large body of water. I need a decent man and an ark. Maybe it can buy me another five thousand years to be a better father."

"No, no. No. No. Emily help me!!!"

"Yes, it's time. I really feel it's time to stir the waters up. I mean just look at this world. You think locking your cars, your houses, your fragile little hearts is normal? You shouldn't need to protect your things from your own employees or worry about neighborhood kids selling your kids drugs, or worse, shooting up the school. That's just the start of it, isn't it? It's gone too far this time. There's going to be a lot of rain. Edward, you're a woodsmith, an inventor. I don't need to tell you how to build a boat -- just make it big enough for you, your family -- bring some women for the boys and for yourself. Bring two of each animal -- I know that can be quite impossible with evolution and all the different little species. Just bring what you can -- I can create the other ones again. That's not hard. But bring some -- it's important for your kids to see. To respect life again. To appreciate life again."

"I don't know. I've never built anything that floats. I'm just a lumberman."

"Oh Jesus. You're fuckin' pathetic," JJ returns to his poltergeist, "Look at you. You're alive! And not that I'm anyone to be takin' tips from, but, the one decent thing I did before I died -- givin' you the yard -- for me, dat was like an infinitely good thing to do. So now, like a guy like you -- you gotta do some huge, like Biblically large scale thing to

get dat same effect -- you being a guy fulla decent deeds an' all," JJ checks his pockets again, "Just one friggin' smoke here?"

Eddie, on his knees in a pool of tears, looks up. JJ is gone. "If I'm so damned decent and you really are God..." a tear falls from his patch to the puddle, "why did you take Emily from me?!!!!!!!"

Eddie's passionate words vibrate the wooden house. Up in Henry's room, the Bible study silences. Henry grimaces in shame, embarrassment and anger.

Day 1

Having awoken in the pre-dawn from a difficult sleep, David sits alone, cross-legged in the bathtub. Water drips from his hair onto Sheila's little boat bobbling in the bath. He stares stupidly at the toy, then in his lonely solitude, makes putt putt noises, pushing it along.

Henry hops off the bus towards the lumberyard. His complacent "ready-to-work" demeanor quickly evaporates upon seeing four tree-sized posts in rectangle formation -- a canvas tarp strapped across and waving at their top.

"What's going on?" Henry speaks without even looking for a person to ask.

Eddie tightens the ropes securing the tarp to the posts. He doesn't answer Henry.

David peeks out from around one of the posts, "Remember the job we were workin' on last week?"

Henry raises an eyebrow, "Yeah...?"

"Forget it. We're clearing a big space then uhm, uhm, making some scaffolding."

"What for?"

Eddie decides to answer, "An ark."

Feeling toyed with, Henry's eyes narrow, "What!?"

Eddie stops what he's doing, walks over and puts his arm around his son, "Jesus, son, I, I,..."

"He saw God." David jumps in, "God told him to build an ark -- you know, like in the Bible."

Tears immediately flood from under Henry's eyes. He slinks out from under Eddie's arm, "Dad!!? What is wrong with you?"

Both David and Eddie are taken aback by Henry's upset, hurt reaction. Eddie, already finding words difficult, is now completely without them.

"No, really." David finally explains, "Your father doesn't shit around."

Henry struggles to dam the waters flowing from his eyes. Soaking his shirt sleeves with tears he finally chokes up enough breath to spit out his reply. "Maybe I should bash your eye out and see if you shit around!" Henry's hurt drifts into anger. He walks away, purposely ramming his shoulder into David's as he takes off down the street.

Eddie gathers his emotions, holding off another cry. David, jaw gaping, watches Henry walk off past the painters whitewashing that huge billboard of JJ.

"Look." Eddie manages a sentence to David, "let's break. I've got a few errands to run on the way home."

Henry, dried streams of tears on his face, gazes out the bus window at the dirty city. Just as he witnesses another car jacking, a flash of lightening momentarily brightens the gray sky. The burst of light makes of the dusty bus window a millisecond x-ray of the world outside. Henry looks up into the darkening clouds then drops his head between his legs. He doesn't notice the hairline fractures, broken bones, broken hearts, nor the cabbage man in the adjacent bus seat, who sits soberly watching him with sympathetic eyes. A single drop

of rain falls on the dry dirty window, cleaning a streak one-millimeter wide.

Day 2

Hidden behind a stack of boating books, Eddie looks up at the library's clock. It's dinnertime. Eddie sighs, scratches his beard and stacks the books under his arm to leave.

Pulling his collar up around his neck, Eddie stashes the library card he borrowed from Japeth back into his pocket. He ducks his head from the drizzle and loads the books behind the driver's seat of his truck.

Day 3

At Bill's Burgers & Doughnuts, just across the street from the JJ/Eddie's lumberyard, David stands on a stool, leaning over the bar, biting into a big sloppy burger dripping from one hand and adjusting the TV antennae with the other hand.

The News: "...Well finally a break in the weather. Don't those first few drops feel great? Let's go upstate with Arny Teller..."

Arny: "Arny Teller here with local farmer Jim Story. How do you feel about this turn of climate?"

Jim: "Well of course it's just great, Arny, just great. The rain is music to our ears."

David stops chewing the mouthful of burger awaiting his chomps. He looks around to see what other people are thinking. Bill, a stout man in his fifties, pulls out a sheet of paper and asks facetiously, "Hey, Davie, you think JJ needs

that billboard anymore?" Bill's voice rattles like that tiny ball in an empty spray paint can.

"What?" David looks over distracted, "Uhm, I guess not."

"After all, it's got my name on it."

"What does?"

"Bill...board! Ha!" Bill proudly shoves some sketch paper over in front of David's face, "See: Rise & Shine at Bill's Burgers & Doughnuts."

David, still with one eye on the TV, "Yeah... rise and shine, that's great."

Japeth chooses his weapon on his favorite computer video game - a machine gun the likes of which even a grown man would have trouble lifting. He blasts bad guys to bloody pieces. Sam sits on the sofa in the living room reading a letter from Jeanie. The letter has a colored-pencil kiss on it.

The TV is on: "...news bad news. Of course, we're all happy about the rain, but some scientists who have been following the effects of the drought are making some unbelievable warnings. Dr Zanter, USC research center..."

Dr. Zanter on TV: "You see, the drought was not just localized in the Midwest. It was the regional symptom of a larger dry warming system. Now, it's clear that that system has run its course, but not without larger effects..."

Henry walks in, kicks Sam to move over on the couch and sits down. Japeth ignores him.

Dr. Zanter: "...Researchers in Canada's Northern Territories have been taking readings of the ground temperatures and water levels ... and well ... to put it quite

simply, the tundra has been thawing, icebergs shrinking. The waters have been rising to some unprecedented levels."

TV newscaster: "Is this dangerous?"

Dr. Zanter: "Well, not at this point, that is, we don't know. The Earth goes through many changes, we've never seen anything like this and we just...

Click.

Henry, hearing dad pull up, switches off the set and storms off to his room, pumped red and mad.

"Hey, I was watching that!" Sam looks up from the letter, reacting to Henry's passive anger.

Eddie steps in, "Whose night is it?"

Sam relaxes his narrowed eyes from Henry's back, brightens up and says, "Yours."

Eddie sighs, "Yeah, that's right..." He pauses, enjoying the uncommon silence of a shut off TV. He looks up and over to his youngest, "Japeth, did you get the internet up yet?"

"I'm surfing now," Japeth mumbles, "One whole free month, and unlimited hours. Wanna know the time in Moscow?"

Eddie steps over to Japeth and the computer, "How about the weather in Moscow?"

"Hold on..." Japeth taps at the keyboard for a few seconds,"60's and rainy."

Eddie sighs, smiles in an uncharacteristically oh-what-the-hell manner, then bursts, "Kids, you like sailing?"

Sam looks up from his letter again, "What?"

Eddie shakes his head at the sheer ridiculousness of what he's about to say to his kids, "Come on, where's Henry? Let's get some fried chicken, I've got a family discussion to lay on you."

David plays with the coiled wire of the phone as he watches the rain pelt against the window of his empty home,

"Babe, I'm not asking you to come back. Look, your father's got that boat up in Cleveland. As long as you're not gonna ah, ah, stay here, why don't you go out there for a while?" David scratches his ear, "And ah, ah, stock that boat real good..."

He listens only partially; most of his attention remains on the storm outside. "I am *not* crazy. And even if Eddie *is* crazy, I'm standing behind him this time." David's man voice breaks into pleading, but this time surprisingly controlled, "Please, please, go to your father's!"

Eddie and all three boys sit in the restaurant with a table full of chicken. Eddie relaxes, and leans back in a chair built for a much smaller person. He's relieved about telling them the big news, and calmly awaits the reaction of his family.

A stunned silence grips the young men, perched and motionless.

Finally, Japeth speaks, "So is that why you asked if we like sailing?"

Henry shrugs, his face is red, he's nearly snarling. Eddie nods an affirmative smile that would normally disarm anyone; he casts a caring eye in Henry's direction.

Sam, hoping dad is joking, pops, "You know you look so serious. I mean, you really look serious...I mean, like you're not joking."

Henry calms himself as best he can, but strongly states what needs to be said. "Dad? Get it together. You took a crowbar to the head two weeks ago. Your boss gets blown away last week. The Bible talks about stress making people crazy like this."

"The Bible talks about an ark too," Sam offers up in a noncommittal, yet diplomatic fashion.

Not surprisingly, Sam's offering only serves to anger Henry all the more, "That was a long time ago. Besides, Dad did not talk to God!"

Sam grunts in a retreating tone, "I was just saying."

Eddie, motivated by the supernatural encounter, simplifies, "I talked to my dead boss. And then your mother. And then that friend of yours that was killed in the train accident. And then I talked to God." Eddie looks at his eldest son, takes a deep breath and finishes, "Henry, he said you'd have trouble with this."

An adamant Henry reiterates, "You did not talk to God!"

Japeth breaks his silence, "It did just start raining like the day after dad uhm, uhm…you know."

"That was coming." Henry deflects, "They've been predicting it for days."

Japeth keeps his reply under breath as to avoid any further barbed words from Henry, "Weeks, more like."

Henry crosses his arms and turns his head away in stubbornness. Sam looks over to his father, awaiting further clarification. Japeth just drops his head down and waits for the discussion to end.

Day 5

Painters work in the drizzle, putting finishing touches on the new ad over JJ's face. "BILL'S BURGERS & DOUGHNUTS -- THIS EXIT." They've left JJ's big smile beaming across the sun face. The resulting image is eerily surreal, ironic with the promise of life and a grinning reminder of death. In front and below the sign, Eddie and David diligently work on the hull of the boat. At the Burgers & Doughnuts across the street, Bill watches the two men constructing something large in the yard.

Japeth and Sam scan products at the local electronics store, particularly researching boating equipment.

Sam skims a note from his dad, the salesman stands ready to help, "We need to look at your...Sounding devices?"

The salesman nods, "You mean depth sounder?"

Japeth perks up, "Yeah, one with a power-savings system and accurate ta within 1.5 feet."

The salesman narrows his eyes toward Japeth, smiles, and takes off to get one in the back.

"What are we doing, Japers?" Sam verbally reaches for reality, "This is crazy."

"Yeah, but we get out of school, and...," Japeth holds up the credit cards, "We got a 25,000 dollar credit line!"

Seven teens sit on the floor in Henry's friend's family living room; Mrs. Jagulski gets cola for them.

"Your father needs help. The Bible says you're supposed to respect your parents," one of the teens says thoughtfully to Henry.

Unsettled, Henry remarks argumentatively, "It also says that you will be betrayed by even your parents and brothers."

Another teen drops his jaw, "Really? Where?" He rustles through the Bible.

The hosting teen offers, "My mom's a school psychologist. Maybe, Maybe..."

"Psychologist?" Henry can no longer gate the tears; he starts to cry. The teens pat him on the back and fall into a group hug.

Day 6

Bill wipes some spilt and dried vanilla shake from the restaurant's glass door, then shifts his focus toward Eddie and David's ominous wood structure. Though it's obviously a boat, Bill's black and white imagination blocks that realization. Similarly, when he looks up toward the freeway and his new billboard, he notices that the boat is blocking his brilliant RISE & SHINE sign from thousands of hungry commuter eyeballs.

The TV is on: "...After a two-week stand off with the police, the woman was finally apprehended today when she stepped out for a walk. Terry W. Garcia locked herself in her house last month after her children acquired a court order for psychiatric testing. When Ms. Garcia refused to honor that order, police tried to enter the house by use of force. The woman shot back at them. They tried tear gas as well..."

Bill, ignoring the TV, tosses the dirty rag at the sink and steps out of his café in a huff. Without hesitation he steps right up to the two woodsmiths and growls roughly, "So, Johnson, watchya building?"

David answers first, "You don't wanna know."

Then Eddie, "A boat."

Bill grimaces, "Christ, right here in the middle of Columbus. Can't you do that somewhere else? *Like near WATER!?*"

"The problem is, I've got a lumberyard here." Eddie throws his hands up.

Bill repositions himself, "The problem is, Johnson ... your fucking boat is blocking my fucking sign!"

David attempts to calm the situation, "Look, it won't be too long."

"You bet it won't!" Bill's got his pointing finger out, "You know how much I'm paying per day for that sign?" He

stumbles off, pissed, but looking up and back over a nervous shoulder as the larger craft splashes an intimidating shadow across his path.

Up, again, burning the midnight oil, Eddie pages through an already worn folder of sketches. His crudely penciled drafts of his ark float between the covers. He closes the folder and lazily looks over all the electronic gadgets the kids have purchased: depth sounder, solar panels, wind generator. With a scratch of the head, he gets up to check on his sleeping children. He carefully steps into the bluish moonlit bedroom of his second son, "Sam? Sam?"

Sam's eyes crack to squints, "Huh, what? Dad?"

"Sam? I want to tell you how proud I am of you...and..."

"Yeah...Sure dad." Sam collects himself.

"I mean, you've been really great with Japer and getting all the equipment...and..."

Sam rubs some sleep from his eyes, "And? What do you need now?"

"This girl, Jeanie ... How do you feel about her?"

This question sobers Sam to full wakefulness, "Dad?"

"Sam, do you love her?"

Now a bit embarrassed, "I don't know."

Eddie, a little embarrassed too, "Have you, uhm, you know?"

"Dad? You mean kissed her?"

Eddie gathers courage, "I mean, I uhm, mean ... made love to her?

"Jesus, no!" Sam backs into his covers, "It took me two weeks just ta tell her I liked her."

"That's... that's... uhm," Eddie smiles, loving his son. "Sam ... God wants her to come."

"What, on your ark?"

"Yeah ... it's gonna take some planning, but..."

"You really *are* serious. Maybe Henry's right, maybe we should get you to see Jagulski's mom, the shrink."

Eddie puts his head down on Sam's chest and hugs him, "Sam, you're gonna have to make a choice. We just don't have the time to work this out all nice."

Sam's Adam's apple suddenly sharply hardens, a stone in the neck of a bird. He begins to weep.

Eddie's eye wells up too, "Now, you're doing real good. Real good. Jeanie, she's a nice girl. You're gonna have ta talk to her parents though," Eddie gathers himself, leans his one eye forward at Sam. He whispers, "And, and when you go to pick up the medical supplies, don't forget lots of gauze and iodine ... and, uhm, you'll need to get some, uhm, contraceptives too."

"Dad???"

"A lot of 'em."

"Dad, I'm fifteen! Besides if God really did tell you to build an ark -- aren't you gonna have to, uhm, ... you know...."

"I don't know how long we'll be floating, son," Eddie's buoyant mood suddenly evaporates. Even in the dim blue light of the room, stormy waves seem to brew in his stone cold serious eyes, "and I absolutely do not want to be birthing any babies at sea."

Sam quiets, "All right dad. Medicine stuff and condoms."

Day 7

David chows down on a Billy Burger, Bill wipes the counter and makes conversation. "It was the PR guy's idea to keep JJ's shit-eating grin."

"Oh, yeah ... on the sign?" David talks with his mouth full, "... Yeah ... that's great ... Come to Bill's and eat some shit."

"No, not like that. Like it might be twisted, he says, but people will look at the sign longer because of it ... you know JJ's smile and all."

A waitress walks up to the TV and turns up the news: "...again to Dr. Zanter."

Dr. Zanter on TV: "Now, we, we're hoping that the new rains would have protected the polar regions from the warming system, but the precipitation isn't snow in these areas, as we would have predicted. It's raining there as well."

Newscaster: "...and this means?"

Bill and David stop their verbal volley and turn their heads toward the tube.

Dr. Zanter: "This means, and I can't believe I'm saying this -- glacier melting. Glacier melting. This could bring global chaos to the weather picture."

Newscaster: "Chaos?"

Dr. Zanter: "Tidal waves...hurricanes...floods."

David points at the TV as if to say "told you so." Bill grunts, shaking his head and pointing at the lumberyard across the street, "I don't care if I'm swimmin' here. That loony friend of yours did not talk to God! And if he doesn't get that fuckin' shipwreck out of JJ's golden smile..."

"You'll what?" David challenges Bill's threat.

Bill shakes his head, tosses the rag into the sink. Muting his disdain he shuts off the TV set.

All three Johnson boys sit on Mrs. Jagulski's sofa, shortest to tallest. Mrs Jagulski, smiles disarmingly, "We all want to do what's best for your dad -- don't we?"

Henry looks over at his younger brothers, determined to win them over, "That's right...right guys?"

Sam has his eyebrows up in confusion and indecision, Japeth stares at the floor as usual.

"Well, yeah, of course, we want to help him, but?" Sam finally responds, no longer able to bare the pressing silence and eyeballs.

"But what?" Henry throws his hands up, "You mean, what if he really is talking to dead guys?"

"Sam," Mrs. Jagulski takes the opportunity, "Henry told me that your father talks to your mother. That he's done it for years."

"Sure, but that's..."

"Sam," Mrs. Jagulski continues, "do you really think out of all the people in the world, God chose your father to talk to?"

"I don't know."

"Are you really prepared to believe that God is going to kill me and my son and all your classmates with a flood ... and that your father alone will survive in an ark?"

Finally Eddie's most diplomatic, resilient child, cracks a few tears, "I don't know."

"I don't mean to be so hard on you, but if Henry is right. Then what do we do a month from now, when the skies clear and your father is so far in debt that he can't possibly care for you guys. You've got no other family -- you'd go to the courts. When he comes to his senses -- it would crush him, wouldn't it?" Mrs. Jagulski, sighs sympathetically with Sam's tears. She gives him a moment then pulls out a document, "This, uhm, is a court order. All it's saying is that your father must undergo psychiatric testing. That's all."

Japeth doesn't break his stare on a crack in the floor, "You're gonna put him in the loony house."

"That's not true Japeth!" Mrs. Jagulski defends, "Lots of people have been tested and just let go to lead normal lives. Henry is going to sign this. We don't need your

signatures, but it would sure help. Not just the courts, but you too."

Henry grabs the paper and deliberately signs it. He shoves the sheet and the pen over to Sam. Sam jams his palms up to his crying eyes, as if pushing on his head long enough would make all of this insanity go away. But the pressure of his own hands is no match for the pressure brewing in the room. He finally dares to open his eyes, hoping against all hope, that everyone has left. But no one has moved, and the weight of their stares caves in his chest -- a sigh escapes him. Sam grabs the pen, signs in a desperate attempt to terminate the awful meeting. He spits the pen out of his hand toward Japeth who still hasn't looked up. Japeth simply shakes his head, he doesn't want any part of it. Now embarrassed, Sam pounds a fist down on the paper and runs out.

Day 8

Droplets of water make a crosshatch pattern in the mud; David and Eddie work in the shower. The timbre of rain, even in the face of the looming threat, sounds good to them after weeks of drought. The smell, the scent of water in the air is still welcome, despite the words that only Eddie Johnson has heard.

"You need sails? Or a motor?" David yells over patter to Eddie.

"I don't know, David. I don't think we'll have time to figure that out. I was just thinking we'd ah, ah, float around, you know, over Ohio or whatever and then when the floods finally, ah ah, dry up -- we'll ... ah ... have some idea of where we are..." Eddie suddenly starts to cry, "where..."

"Eddie?"

"This is crazy, David, absolutely insane. What? We're just gonna bobble there like a fucking duck?"

"It's okay Eddie, don't slip on me now, you're not going crazy alone."

"Everybody dies, David … Everybody."

David pauses, but discards the big picture rumination in exchange for keeping Eddie sane. Easing into an awkward smile, David humors, "They're all a bunch of assholes anyway."

"You too?"

"Christ Eddie, I got your eye knocked outta yer head."

"And Henry?"

"Henry? Whaddya mean Henry?"

"JJ … I mean, God, paid me another visit last night. He said …ahm … they said..." Eddie sniffles and wipes his nose with his filthy forearm, "Leave Henry..."

"What? Leave Henry here?"

Eddie nods.

David loses his ability to humor, "Don't worry Eddie, I'll watch after him."

Eddie shakes his head, "They said, God said, to take *you* instead."

Completely stymied, David takes a weak step backward, it's the first time that he actually believes Eddie. This idea of a flood finally *sinks* in to David's thick motionless skull, the rain drips down his face.

Across the street, Bill stands outside his store, peeping from under an umbrella up at his glorious sign and the boat that's blocking it from the freeway. A truck charges passed and swashes a large quantity of water on him. "Jesus!" Bill grumbles some obscenities, but the size and depth of the surrounding puddles quiets him.

Sam mopes along in the rain, dragging his feet through the puddles. He passes a group of people trying to drain their basement with buckets and siphon hoses. His eyes widen in worry and he picks up the pace of his saunter almost to a run.

A magazine rack at the local drugstore hosts a myriad of headlines: "Man Rapes 70-Year-Old Nun," "Bomb Kills 8 soldiers," "Gang Fight Leaves 5-Year-Old Dead." Standing in front of the dismal news, a clerk at the register watches a TV set mounted near the ceiling to the right of three security monitors. Below the register a shotgun is mounted.

Newscaster: "... No relief in sight for these record-breaking rains. And let me tell you something folks, I've been in the meteorology business for twenty-five years -- I've never seen it rain everywhere in the world at once. Right here at home in the US, the flood damage total is rising prompting the president to release one billion dollars in emergency funds and caution us with these simple prevention measures..."

Sam steps up to the counter with an armful of gauze and various ointments. He waits silently for the clerk to turn around.

Newscaster: "Make sure all your drainage pipes are clear, have them rotored, clear your curbs of leaves and other debris."

The clerk turns to Sam, keeping one eye on the set, "Yeah?"

Sam drops all that stuff on the counter prompting a rise of the clerk's eyebrows, "Planning a skateboarding field trip?"

"I don't know how to skateboard," Sam hesitantly pulls the box of condoms from under his elbow, "Uhm, uh, you got anymore of these?"

The clerk sharply lowers those eyebrows, "How many more?"

"Fifty more..."

"Fifty?"

"Fifty more, ... *boxes.*"

The clerk gives Sam a long hard look then reaches under the counter.

Newscaster: "...and as an added safety precaution, pick up one of those inflatable rafts, or small fishing boats -- something with oars."

Sam hands the clerk Eddie's credit card and turns his head away.

The clerk rings up the products, "How old are you?"

"Fifteen"

The clerk scratches his head, "Looks like I was way off about that skateboarding..."

Eddie's front hall is cluttered with dripping raincoats, boots, and umbrellas. A path of damp sock marks track to the dining room where the Johnson family sits deathly quiet at the dinner table. Exhausted and hungry, a little scared, the only sounds they make are eating related. Japeth finishes first and waits at least two minutes for someone to look up from their food. Finally, he speaks anyway, lowering his head just a bit to fit in, "I got a bunch of CDs & DVDs: Music and movies... 'T2' in digital surround!"

Henry looks up, pissed.

"Good thinkin' there Japer," Eddie acknowledges in between chomps, "It could get pretty boring. I mean, I didn't thinka that."

Sam puts his glass down, "I got the medical supplies, and, and, those other things you asked me to."

Henry turns his evil eye to Sam.

"Great, son, that's great." Eddie headnods, "I, uh, David and me are gonna be done with the outside of the boat

soon. I stopped by and picked up some books from the library too."

Japeth offers, You can get those on CD. They'll take up less room and weigh a lot less."

Eddie, truly impressed with his son's knowledge, "You're one sharp sharp kid, Japeth. Your mother would've been so proud of you."

That one last unbearable sentence smacks Henry into a deliberate stand. He dumps his dish in the sink and retreats to his bedroom. The three remaining Johnsons sit silently as Henry's storming footsteps make their way up the stairs, crescendoing with a door slam.

"This is not going to be easy." Eddie cautions in an oddly comforting tone.

Sam, lost in his own worries, remarks, "What? You mean Jeanie's parents?"

Japeth pops, "Jeanie's coming?"

Eddie sighs looking at his two youngest sons, "Oh yeah, that..." he drops his chin into his hand, elbow propped on the wooden table, "And then there's the animals."

Japeth mutters, swirling his spoon around in his mashed potatoes, "Two by two."

Eddie nods, "Two by two."

A long pause blankets the table like linen. Almost fearful, but woven too tightly with inconceivability for any real fright.

"Oh yeah, too" Japeth pops away from the table and digs into his backpack, "I also got you one of these."

Sam's curiosity gets the better of him, and he drops Jeanie meditations for the wire-bound book in Japeth's hand, "A diary?"

Japeth hands the book to Eddie, "No, a log. You know like on 'Star Trek.' You're the captain. You'll need a captain's log."

Eddie rolls his eyes, "Captain?"

Day 9

Japeth and friend Jimmy sit up on one mighty branch of a mammoth oak tree. Jimmy holds an umbrella over Japeth who dangles half a carrot in front of a suspicious little squirrel.

"You know, I think squirrels aren't into carrots, Japer." Jimmy scratches his leg.

"Yeah, you got any nuts?"

"Nope, maybe we should try to catch a rabbit?"

The two boys lazily nod their heads in unison. A crow looks on from across the tree, hiding from the rain beneath a leafy branch.

Jape looks down at the large puddles. "Don't suppose we'll have to catch any fish."

Jimmy continues the headnodding, "Nope."

Gathering up his angst, and trudging through the now six inches of water, a tooth-gritting Bill Battlon hobbles up to David and Eddie, who persistently pound nails into the wooden craft. "You know, Johnson, your fucking 'ark' is still blocking my fucking sign!"

"Won't be long." Eddie doesn't even look up from his work. "Don't worry."

"God damn right it won't be long. I got less customers than when I put the damn thing up."

"I'm still eating there," David reassures.

"Next week, I'm ordering 30 burgers," Eddie consoles, "To go!"

"Eddie, this is real life," Bill takes a more compassionate, yet firm tone, "I called the city. You got no fuckin' building permit. And with JJ in the ground, no friends

in high places. I'm not kidding, I'm pullin' the plug on your little toyboat charade."

"Real kind-hearted of you, Bill. You're a Samaritan." David defends, "They'll fine him first, he won't pay, then they'll summon him, he won't go. Then they'll come to arrest him in a couple of months. Believe me, I know firsthand how all that crap goes down. By that time, you and your sign will be fifty feet underwater."

Bill shakes his head, "You're both lunatics. My brother in-law's an alderman in the sixth district. I'll have you outta here in three days."

Eddie stops his banging and looks directly at Bill for the first time during this discussion. He's quieted and surprised by Bill's harsh threats, "Did you ever stop to think that you might be losing customers because they're stuck at home bailing their basements?"

Bill looks down at the ground, a bit ashamed to have to use such drastic measures, but to him, Eddie is obviously out of his mind. As if to spare Bill the bother of introspection, an SUV pulls up and Mrs. Jagulski steps out with a lawyer. She pulls out a document protected in a clear plastic folder. "Mr. Johnson, I've been speaking to your sons."

Both Eddie and Bill turn their concerned attentions toward her. She continues, "The testing won't take long, just a couple of hours. Why don't you take a break? We can use my car."

Bill grunts, "Jesus, Eddie, looks like you've got bigger problems than me."

"Henry's friend Bobbie, you're his mom, aren't you?" Eddie chooses to ignore her attempted intervention.

"Told you he was a loon." Bill snorts toward David and trudges off.

Mrs. Jagulski waves the plastic protected document. "Mr. Johnson, aren't you concerned about your kids?"

"Yeah." Eddie's confidence turns a bit sad, "Could you look after Henry? He's a good kid, a good kid. Just… You'll need a boat. Promise me you gotta boat."

Mrs. Jagulski's eyes well up with pity towards this pathetic man. After a pause, she ruffles through her documents. "I've got a court order, Eddie. If you don't come with me now, I'll come back with the sheriff. They'll arrest you -- that won't be good for the kids."

"You want me to tell my kids that I didn't talk to God, when I know that I did? Lying wouldn't be good for my kids." Eddie appeals to her one more time, "Look, Henry, he won't come -- I know he won't. You're a good woman. I mean Bobbie's a good kid. Take care of Henry for me. Take care of Henry."

Mrs. Jagulski plops the documents on David's chest and shuffles off. David looks down, brushes the water off the plastic, "This looks pretty official Eddie. Signed and stamped by Judge Bernard Gadar."

"By who?" the name of the Judge strikes him out of his thoughts.

"Judge Bernard Gadar or.."

"Gadeer." Eddie cracks a smile.

Japeth paddles an inflatable pool raft through flooded streets. With the water level up to car doors by now, only a few vehicles are still around. A big-wheeled pick-up truck spins its back wheels. Japeth looks up at it as he calmly drifts by.

David steps into Bill's Burgers & Doughnuts. He shuts the door quickly to keep outside water from getting in.

"Better get a real job Davie," Bill starts right in. "That ark thing is crazy."

Uncharacteristically abandoning his street diplomacy, David snaps, "Shut up and give me a goddamn Billy burger."

Surprised at David's tone, Bill tosses a raised eyebrow in that general direction and flips on the TV set. The diner is empty of any other customers.

Newscaster: "'Move to higher ground' that's the latest from the White House. Huge portions of Indiana and Northern Ohio are flooded -- to the tops of trees in some areas. Homes, cars, pets are being left behind as drenched residents flee to the highlands area in the south and even as far west as Missouri..."

His socks and shoes soaked to the bone, Bill mutters under his breath, "I sure to hell hope that boss of yours *is* crazy."

Eddie drives his truck through the two-foot high street flooding and stops at the Gadeer residence. Donning rubber fishing trousers and suspenders, Eddie steps directly into the thigh-high waters and makes his way up the front steps. He knocks and is lead into the house by Mrs. Gadeer's servant. Eddie notices that all of the furniture has been removed. The place is damp and empty. Kelly Gadeer holds a cell phone to her hip welcoming Eddie with a smile.

"Well hello, tall, dark and moral." Mrs. Gadeer's cheery sarcasm contrasts the dismal mansion. "What have I misplaced this time?"

Eddie hands her the document, "You said if I ever needed anythin'."

Kelly keeps her smile, scans the paper, lifts the phone to her cheek. "Uh, Jim, can I call you back?" She hangs up. "Didn't you have two eyes last time I saw you?"

Eddie, "Yes ma'am."

"Ma'am?" Kelly shakes her head, "Am I that old? Anyway...despite the fact that you probably only see half as well, *you still look good.*"

Eddie misses her compliment.

Kelly dons her reading glasses. As she gives the documents another glance, her smile only brightens, "Ha! I knew you were nuts! ... Who else would return a purse with two thousand dollars in cash?"

Eddie, confounded by her reaction, says nothing. The corner of Kelly Gadeers lipstick red mouth curls up into an admiring grin.

Eddie chokes up a sentence, "I'm building an ark. They think I'm crazy -- they said they'd take my kids."

"Look, the only thing this proves," Kelly waves the paper nonchalantly, "Is that my husband got something else done today -- besides his secretary."

Eddie reprises his bewilderment.

Kelly, truly impressed with Eddie's silly resolve and profound innocence, says reassuringly, "This is nothing. don't worry, I'll take care of it." Kelly pauses. Looking Eddie straight in the eye, she chuckles, "Eddie's Ark."

Day 11

Mrs. Beth Hanson, Jeanie's mom, yells down to her husband and son who are in the basement, bailing and rescuing family photos, old gifts, and various other items of sentimental or immediate practical use, "Dan, Roy! Take a break, guys! It's dinner time."

Beth turns back to Jeanie and Sam who are sitting quietly yet uncomfortably at the dinner table. Sam salivates at all the wonderfully prepared food laid out carefully, each entrée with its own serving dish, all the silverware matching. Beth looks over the table, making sure she hasn't forgotten

anything, "It'll be just a second, kids. Oh, I'll get some drinks."

Dan and his son Roy shuffle in. Removing their dripping clothes, they find their seats at the table. Beth would normally remind them to first wash their hands, but given the circumstances, she simply pours some drinks and sits too. There's an awkward silence -- awkward for Sam. Then the family bows their heads in unison.

Dan closes his eyes hard, "Thank you Father for this food ... I know it was quite a job for Beth on a day like today to get it all together, but she did, so we want to thank her and we give thanks for having Sam over with us tonight."

Dan opens his eyes and lifts his head up, triggering Roy's dig into the food. Dan reaches for the roast chicken, "So, Sam what is it that you needed to talk to us about?" He chortles, "You want to marry my Jeanie before she even finishes school?"

The Hansons don playful smiles around the table.

Sam clears his throat, determinedly. "My dad is building an ark. He said God told him to do it and that it's going to rain and not stop until all the earth is covered. He said God told me to bring Jeanie."

As if frozen in time, the Hansons pause mid chew. Even Roy puts his gluttony on hold. He slowly turns his head to Sam, applesauce dripping from his lips. Deathly silently, Sam avoids their impossibly focused eyes. Instead he stares at a cuckoo clock above the mantle, the pendulum swinging back and forth. The Hansons are silent for ten full swings.

Suddenly, Dan coughs into a chuckle, spitting out a piece of half-chewed chicken, then finally bursts into full out laughter. Roy follows.

Mrs. Hanson tilts her head, as a teacher to a child who's just told an off-color joke. "Samuel, you shouldn't use the Lord's name in vain like that."

Jeanie's not laughing, she doesn't get the joke. She's concerned, but not offended. In fact, in some very peculiar way -- complimented.

Beth gets up, giving a 'shame on you look' to Dan and the snickering Roy on her way to the TV. "Let's see what's on the TV." She flips on the tube in hopes of finding a new topic of discussion.

Newscaster: "Teen gives birth at prom, drops baby in the toilet and returns to the dance. Stay tuned for the top story, 'Move to higher ground.' The Midwest and Plains States struggle to keep their heads above water -- and the picture isn't drier anywhere else…"

Beth immediately flips off the set, this time the Hanson silence lasts for only three seconds. Beth Hanson attempts a nervous smile, then snarls through it, "I don't care if we have to climb the Alps! You're not taking my daughter on that Goddamn ark."

Day *12*

The Burger & Doughnut place flooded up to the countertop's height, Bill sits cross-legged in solitude atop the serving bar. He looks up at the ark through his window. David, in a canoe, rows right through the open front door and alongside the bar.

A defeated Bill mumbles, "No doughnuts today, Davie."

"Yeah, Bill, I know, come on, let's go." David pats Bill's back, "You got family in Arlington, don't you?"

Bill silently climbs into the canoe. As the two row off Bill gazes up at the ark looming in front of them. Behind, JJ's smiling-sun billboard hasn't enough strength to rise and shine through the darkening skies. The scent of damp wood filters through the moist air.

Deathly serious, Bill asks, "Have we really been that bad?"

Heavy, infinitely deep, dark gray clouds can barely be seen through the relentless water pellets, making a cheese grater out of the surface of the flood. David diligently rows speechlessly through what is now a shallow lake, very few people are still around. Rooftops are now more often seen than front doors.

Teeth loaded with nails, Eddie hammers a few more into the boat's deck. He sighs to himself, "She's gettin' there. She's really getting there."

David, alone in the canoe, rows up, "What about water? We can't drink sea water," he yells at Eddie.

"It's not sea water -- it's rain water. Right?" Eddie shrugs, "Or will it mix?"

"I don't know."

Eddie nods his head, knowing any amount of thought just won't resolve the many problems they're embarking into. "How about your wife?"

"Eddie, I don't know. I'd stay back with her -- if I knew where she was."

Eddie continues his thoughtless nodding, then, struggling for something encouraging…"Have faith."

David looks up steel-faced, then breaks into cynical laughter.

Eddie fails in an attempt to avoid laughing at himself as well. The two laugh themselves out, then Eddie shakes his head. "You got any better ideas?"

David returns to his newly discovered no-nonsense, getting-down-to-business demeanor, "Yeah, I'll go get the food supplies and some water." He rows off.

The city of his childhood now under between five and fifteen feet of water, David rows past the tops of trucks and trees. The occasional citizen on a raft or fishing boat floats by. They might make eye contact with each other, but no one has the energy or good-humor any more for salutations or well wishing. David drifts into an abandoned supermarket and dives for canned foods.

He packs the canoe to capacity and rows away.

A rescue boat floats by in the other direction. The rescue skipper shouts out to him, "Hey, guy, you're headed the wrong way, 'higher ground' it's west -- past Arlington."

"Yeah, thanks." David's resolve contrasts the skipper's surprise and concern, "Take care."

The skipper calms, narrows his eyes, his head turning on his neck to watch David row off in the distance. He turns his head back to the deck full of cold shivering citizens awaiting higher ground.

David's face is expressionless against the downpour.

"Hey David!" Sam shouts as he and Japeth row alongside in an identical canoe. Only instead of canned food, cages of little animals fill theirs. Sam rowing, Japeth bangs at his handheld video game wrapped in a plastic bag.

"Hey, good goin' guys." The two boys and veritable floating mini-zoo lighten David's mood. David happily breaks from his steadfast mission, he leans over and rubs his finger along the scaly head of a foot long lizard, "Cool, iguanas. I love those things."

Japeth, however, looks upset, still with his head down, "The whole pet store was under. Can you believe they didn't even open the cages and let the puppies out?"

David sighs, his reprieve too soon evaporates. The three in two canoes row up to Eddie at the ark. Eddie has already spotted them at a distance. He's cracking his back watching their approach.

"Great! Let's load them up." Eddie lends his hand, "It won't be too much longer; we'll stay here until she starts to float."

"What about our women, Eddie?" David bursts, "We're just a bunch of men and some iguanas!"

"I don't know, David. Just hand me the next box, would ya?"

Frustrated and becoming angry, David restates his point. "What good is it if we can't make babies?"

Eddie motions again with his hand, "David, the next box, please?"

A crow sidesteps along the railing of the ark.

Barely a hint of the moon's broken glow wafts through portholes across cages cluttering the deck: a couple of turtles, two white mice, iguanas, parakeets, and yes, a couple of squirrels, but not much more. Sam and Japeth asleep on the cabin deck next to them. Eddie is on his back, in his bed area, asleep and snoring softly, a photo of Emily in his hand. David is up in his bed, gently sobbing, a photo of his family in his hands. The rain's pattering drowns out Eddie's snores. On the wooden floor, a box of nails, serving as a paperweight, rests heavily on a drawing of the ark Eddie had sketched out only a handful of days prior.

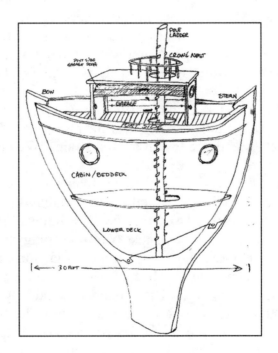

Day 14

Bam! Bam! Pounding on the outside of the ark awakens the two men, the two boys, and the two of everything else. Eddie pops his one eye open. He gathers his senses, unaccustomed to facing a new day from these surroundings. He searches for a dry jacket and throws it on as he ascends to the deck. In the waters below, he finds a fishing boat with the Hanson family aboard. Beth wraps herself tightly, cross-armed in a green-hooded rain jacket. A somber Dan Hanson speaks, "This is Jeanie's choice, not mine."

Jeanie steps up the scaffolding carrying only a flute case. Sam joins Eddie looking over the rail.

Beth's tears are lost in the thick rain, "We don't know what else to do."

Without a word from the Johnsons, the Hansons motor away. Eddie, Sam and Jeanie watch the Hansons' lowered heads drift passed the few remaining rooftops and JJ's shit-eating grin, it too, just barely keeping head above water. Bill's painted sun cracks in the visual some sick joke against the dark, nearly black, waterlogged day. David rushes out to the deck. His anticipation quickly turns to disappointment as no one has come for him. Eddie, Jeanie and Sam return to the dry cabin below. David drowns his sorrow with rain, then with nerve-racking resurgence, his eyes light up again as another boat approaches with what looks like a woman and two children. But the deluge blurs. David wipes the rain from his eyes.

The small boat pauses alongside. David's excitement drops from him like an anchor. The woman is not Sue. The children aren't even children.

The woman speaks with an optimism rivaling David's mood, "Mr. Johnson. Mr. Johnson?"

David turns the back of his head to the woman and yells down from the deck into the ark's cabin, "Eddie!"

The woman grabs some scaffolding as her boat knocks against the ark. Eddie joins David on deck.

"Mr. Johnson?" The woman asks again.

"Yeah?" Eddie yells down.

"I'm Irene Coleman, from the Columbus Ecological Zoo."

"Yeah?"

"Is it true?" Irene Coleman, neck cricking up, eyes blinking to see through the rain, "Did God really talk to you?"

"Yeah."

Irene rolls back a tarp revealing two white cougar cubs licking the rain from their whiskers, "Then, could you take these babies? They're practically tame. I raised them myself."

"Are you a veterinarian?"

"Something like that."

"Well then maybe you'd better come too." Eddie smiles, turns and winks toward David, "There's your woman."

"I'm married!" David retorts, tired of the emotional toggling. "Besides she's your age."

Eddie smiles again, "I'm married too."

Impatiently, the woman yells up again, "Look, just take the cats. I don't think, I..."

Eddie interrupts her plea, talking loudly down to her and with finality, "No veterinarian lady, no cats." His head is directed to her, but his one eye is fixed smilingly on David.

Irene sighs, shakes her head, drops her hands, more frustrated with losing the argument than being forced to board this hopelessly imperfect, not to mention, ugly excuse for a vessel. Still, Irene is no coward, she ties her boat to the

scaffolding and begins to climb up. David and Eddie hoist the cougars.

As if on cue, a sudden wave like the shoulder of some huge buffalo, shoves the mighty ark off its scaffolding. The craft begins to float. The push sends Eddie and David stumbling to the opposite side.

Along with the tip of that wave, confusion splashes across the deck. Eddie and his inexperienced crew struggle with the simple tasks of footing and equilibrium for several seconds. The ship floats listlessly right through Bill's beautiful billboard, shredding the smiling sun into soaked shards of paper.

Finally, Eddie catches his balance and is able to concentrate on obstacles off the boat, he focuses on some treetops about 100 yards off to the right, "Japeth get that sounder going!"

David grabs a two-by-four, bracing it against the top of a telephone pole; he struggles to keep the boat from bumping into it. Sam lends a hand. Eddie picks up a plank as well, scouting for the next hurdle. Swirling waters push them toward the center of the city, the ark's bottom scraping against submerged rooftops, each time sending a bone-jarring vibration through the inexperienced crew. One tall office building catches Eddie's eye. He scrambles for the boat's anchor, still new and in the box, "If we can tie her onto that building there, it'll buy us some time while the water level increases. I don't want to ram this thing into one more rooftop!"

No one counters. Jeanie and Sam help out with the "jousting," pointing at the sinking building with their pick-up sticks. Japeth brings the sounder up on deck, he's got the directions out, reading them furiously. Irene checks below on the other animals. Eddie tears the anchor out of the box, grabs a shiny new rope tying it through the anchor's hole and then to the boat's center pole. He looks at his knot with hands

up and out, like an apprentice magician casting a new spell. He turns toward David, "You know anything about knots?"

David shakes his head "no." Sammy and Jeanie follow suit. The office building swiftly approaches; the skinny crew, doing a satisfactory job of pushing off other structures, has aimed the boat well. All three prop their sticks toward the building and attempt to soften the bump. Eddie grabs the rope just two feet from the anchor, rocking it back and forth like a pendulum, readying for a toss into the unbroken windows of the building's 17th floor. Three sticks poke the building, Sammy, Jeanie, David bracing. Eddie's last windup is interrupted only by the physics of inertia, wood to steel, which sends Eddie right over the railing and through the window -- anchor and all. Jeanie tentatively screams. David steadies the boat as best he can with that one stick, then looking into the broken window, "Eddie?"

Eddie, now laying in the office building still holding the anchor, gets up and pops his scratched head back out the window, "I got the anchor through on my first shot," he humors, and ties the boat snugly to the short skyscraper.

Having successfully anchored the clumsy little ark, the crew takes a well-deserved breath of air, save for the agitated David, who steps away from the group. He crashes a window three over from Eddie's with his two-by-four. Climbing deeper into the deserted office space, David plops himself down in a cubicle.

On deck, Irene turns to Jeanie. "Rather ironic -- don't you think?"

"What?" Jeanie's eyes don't show much interest in Irene's verbal tease.

"Tying Eddie Johnson's ark to an office building."

"Yeah, why?"

"Well, I don't know, kind of like, or at least for me, this is a floating ark of faith strapped onto a symbol of the

corporate conservative standard of a secure life. It's just ironic."

Jeanie shakes her head at Irene and turns disrespectfully away, "Yeah, whatever."

Like the building itself, abandoned and left in disarray, David grumbles, grabs a newspaper sprawling over a desk full of forms and applications. Headline: "Move to Higher Ground." The photo of a harbor full of demolished ships is captioned: Coastal Hurricanes Tear Up Naval Vessels. David huffs, he leans back, tosses his feet up on the desk, and reaches into his pocket for Sheila's little boat. His anger leaves him that instant, replaced by tears. David brings the little boat to his lips, kisses it and closes his eyes in sweet dangerous memory. Then, upon opening them again, a cracked glass photo of a family separates itself from the other scattered desk items. David wipes some dust away from it. A man, a women, a boy, a girl, a dog. Your standard everyday average family. David wonders where this family has scurried off to, if at all. Would they find a way out of the flood? Or would they simply perish? What had they done so deserving of suffocation by water?

Eddie's boat holds to the building like a bobber on a fisherman's line -- a fetus at full term, passing out of its mother's womb, both hands on the umbilical cord. A painful clutching grip, as one clenches his or her way of life -- regardless of its value -- a clench.

"David! David!"

David quickly puts the boat back into his pocket and turns.

Sam is shouting through the broken window, "David! David!"

"What?" David replies annoyed.

Sam's silhouette can be seen at the broken window. "Get over here! Come over here now!"

David takes a second to strongly wipe away any trace of crying from his face. He composes himself and, with a resolve becoming more and more descriptive of his constitution, he steps briskly toward the window, ready to face and charge the latest immediate crisis. Sam has already left the window. David grabs the top of the window frame and powerfully hops through onto the boat. He inhales sharply through his nose, "Whadya need Sam?"

Sam points down at the surface of the water to a National Guard boat populated by a few officers and a dozen or so damp rescuees. The ship's officer speaks, "David MacMay?"

Eddie answers, "Yeah, we got one a those."

David peers over the railing. "Sue!"

Eddie and the officer assist Sue with little Sheila as they climb from the Guard boat to Eddie's ark.

"She insisted we take her here," The officer gives a skeptical eye to this floating hunk of lumber and then echoes the skepticism verbally to Eddie. "You're not expecting to spend any serious time afloat in this thing, are ya?"

Eddie looks over the sad faces of drenched civilians still in the National Guard Rescue boat. Eddie's expression echoes that skepticism once more, but this time in the direction of the Guard's craft. "You're not seriously expecting to dock some place, are ya?"

Puzzled, the National Guard floats off.

David hugs Sue tightly, like a tree grips the ground, like gravity holds things to earth, like a boat to an anchor. "The anchor!" David kisses little Sheila on the nose and looks over Sue's shoulder. The ark has ascended to the top of the building in the rapidly rising waters and storm. "Eddie, we gotta let go a this building!"

Eddie, gathering courage and a knife, "Yeah. I know."

They struggle to pull the anchor up, but it's caught and tangled down on the 17th floor.

"Cut it, Eddie! Cut it, or it'll pull us under!"

Eddie considers the slack left on the line and the rate of the rising water.

Eddie looks around for any oncoming obstacles, but all are submerged, save for the swiftly sinking top of this building. "I'm at the end of my rope!" Eddie yells out, laughing a scary laugh, perhaps a tapdance with insanity. Then, with one sharp jab, he cuts the anchor line.

The coil snaps, echoing angrily against the sound of the nailing rain. The boat wails an awful visceral groan to be at real sea. Wood cracking like ribs, its cry eclipses David's sigh of relief, but gives voice to Eddie's heartbreak. Eddie slips down to one knee. His eye fixes behind, docking on that one office building slowly shrinking in the drifting wake. Seemingly sinking. Seemingly sinking. It's Henry. It's Bill. It's Joe. It's the last sight of the way things were. But mostly, to Eddie, it's Henry.

$\mathcal{D}ay$ $\mathit{15}$

On beddeck, Eddie wakes alone, save for the cages of animals and supplies that were never properly stored. A nauseous grunt knocks him into consciousness. He holds both his big hands down on the bed as if to stop the boat from rocking. Then he stumbles warily up the pole ladder to deck. The sky is gray and cloudy, but at least not so dark, and the rain has quieted to a drizzle. He promptly shuffles to the railing and heaves. He vomits again, then looks down the railing to see David heaving also, and further down Sue and Sheila, and Irene with Sam and Japeth who also look like they've had their heave and are trying quietly to recover.

David coughs to a regurgitation conclusion, wipes a half digested bit from his lips. "First hand, Davie MacMay reporting, Sir."

Eddie tosses the last of his stomach's contents, picks some water up off the deck and splashes it on his own face. He slides to a sitting position on the deck, back against the railing, and looks out and over to see nothing but water, ocean. He looks back at David and starts to chuckle. David joins him. The others look on, too nauseated to do or say anything. Eddie's laughs climax to a sort of sick laughter, twisted, the laughter of a person pressured to howl, so burdened with preposterousness that sound mind must finally be lifted from its cradle of protection and set free -- jettisoned. Eddie, for sure on the brink of extracting sanity from his soul, finally opts to keep it, despite the obvious impossibility to follow. The laughter stutters to sobs, then full fledged crying. David's grin dampens to a frown. He sobs also, but not to the depth of Eddie's wailing. Barely enough energy left to breathe, David watches Eddie drop his head in his hands.

Sam and Japeth look away in embarrassment; they're not used to seeing their strong father weep. Irene, cuddling with them, reaches awkwardly to pat Eddie on the shoulder. The wet and wary crew sit in the drizzle, gathering up their scruples which pock the deck like drops of rain.

The sobbing eventually wrings Eddie dry, inflaming his throat and knotting his neck like anchor rope. He suddenly and sharply inhales, then coughs. "Come on," he spits out. This self-directed command becomes an invitation as Eddie remembers the others aboard. "Come on, let's get those animals outta our beddeck; bring 'em down to the lower one." With one look into David's concerned eyes, Eddie realizes just how much his lamenting has shaken the others. One more deep breath, Eddie rubs his face into a

forced smile. "Sleeping with the lot of you smelly boneheads is bad enough."

Not quite sure how to respond to Eddie, everyone chooses not to.

"I'll go." David finally relaxes. "You look like you could use a few more minutes to catch your breath -- *Captain.*"

David steps down.

Eddie takes notice of Irene with his kids, "Thank you, Irene."

"Aye, aye Captain." Irene swallows hard. "*Thank you.*"

Down on beddeck, David opens the hatch to the lower deck and takes a tentative stride down into the dark. After five steps his foot is in water. Though he's nearly soaked to the bone from the drizzle on deck, somehow the water in the lower deck is colder and chills his foot to near frozen. Frozen halfway through the hatch, he catches his breath and rummages up a flashlight to investigate further. Even through the light of the dim 3-volt bulb, David can plainly see, at the front of the ship, a limb of a tree has broken through the wood. It's sticking out of the pool of water, twigs, leaves and all. The leak has filled the bottom of the ark with over a foot of water and it's slowly rising. David flips the flashlight off and runs back up to deck.

"Ah, Eddie," David starts as unalarming as possible, "we got a problem."

Eddie, knowing his return to reality would be riddled with problems, pulls himself up to his feet. "Okay, let's have a look."

The two climb back down to the lower deck.

"We could rip it out and patch it with some extra wood or something," David thinks out loud.

"No. We don't got much extra wood," Eddie answers after some thought. "Plus, if this thing is stickin' four feet into my boat -- what's stickin' out the other side?"

In the water outside, David pops his head above the surface and takes a deep breath. He hollers up to the crew leaning over the rail watching, "Yep, it's sticking out about two feet here."

Eddie duct tapes a hand saw to the end of a garden hose and lowers that end down to David. David grabs the saw, detaches it, then experiments with breathing through the hose under water. He reappears after half a minute under, "Garden hose snorkeling, in one easy lesson." The raindrops pop into his blinking eyes.

Eddie focuses on the task at hand. "Actually, it's a good thing -- the limb. Saw it off. We can use it to patch the holes on the inside. Leave three inches or so."

"You sure you don't want me to pull it out?"

"What's the point? It's stopping the water."

David shrugs and takes another dive. Underwater, and biting the end of the hose, he saws off the branch. Small saw dust particles create submerged floating clouds, like a dream, or miso soup. He looks up through the dream to the water's surface to see Sue and Sheila's refracted image lazily warping.

Meanwhile, Irene and Jeanie carry buckets of water from the lower deck to the upper deck and dump them over the edge. Eddie helps his sons with a manual water pump hooked up to another set of garden hoses. The combination of methods is working; the water in the lower deck begins to deplete.

David climbs back on board much to Sue's relief. He kisses Sheila, then cuts the branch chunk into smaller patching pieces. He descends decks, holding a flashlight for

Eddie who's kneeling in the water, manually drilling screws through David's new patching pieces and into the boat. Suddenly, the broken, bent branch shifts like a sick horse whose leg has just given out. Water rushes in. Eddie hurries the patching process, but the water level in the lower deck continues to rise until the two men can no longer see the tools in their hands. The water up to their ears, they cock their heads back like birdlings squawking to be fed. Irene and Sue quicken their bailing pace, as do the boys with the pump.

"I'm not helping here." David stands, "I'll go get you a hose and let you dive."

David climbs off and returns just in time The lower deck is completely under. Eddie waiting at the hatch for the hose, grabs it from David. "If I'm not back in five minutes, tell God he should have commissioned a real boat builder."

With that, Eddie Johnson wraps his mouth around the hose, takes a breath and goes under. David breathes heavily as if for the both of them. He shines the little flashlight down into the deck hole, but the water seems to have made friends with the dark. Black and undaunted by hurried bailing, the water crawls up through the hatch into beddeck. Irene steps down with her empty bucket and gasps. David stands motionless holding the hose and flashlight.

Sleeping cougars wake with the invading waterline. They drowsily step a paw or two back, bobbing their heads in confusion. Though the deck has plenty of animals, human and otherwise, not a peep in the weighted silence.

Eddie's head finally breaks the water's surface, donning an unexpected smile.

"Well?" David pops.

"Well?" Eddie catches his breath. "I still think God should have found someone else," the water encroachment abates, "but I actually might have stopped that damn leak."

David shakes his head into a grin, "Good! Then let's get some of those burgers & doughnuts -- I'm starving." David tosses the hose and heads toward the food storage.

Eddie crawls up into the puddles up on beddeck, the water below recedes with his displacement. Lying on his back, Eddie sucks some fresh air into his tired lungs.

This second night afloat, an exhausted crew in beddeck disarray snore in a sleep deeper than the water over Columbus, Ohio. Soggy bedding under unconscious bodies, animals in cages and not; they sleep where they had earlier stood, legs entangled, like drunkards at a party that never intended to end, save for the instability of human consciousness.

Day 16

Gathering in the deck garage (so named because it resembles a small garage in shape, and is fitted with two garage doors facing either side of the craft), the group sits around a gas camping grill, drinking coffee and eating pancakes.

"So, so ..." Irene worries that her question might be a tad stupid, "How long? I mean how long can we expect to be sailing?"

The rest of the crew, deeming it a very good question turn their heads in the direction of Eddie.

"I'm not sure." Eddie answers without looking up from his pancakes.

Content to find that her first question wasn't followed by a foul answer, Irene continues the line, "And the plan? Do we head somewhere? Chart a course or whatever?"

David, happy to know the answer, replies, "No, we've decided to just float. I mean, we didn't have time for a sail or a motor; we didn't know where to go anyway."

Not quite the profound blueprint she was hoping for, a gracious Irene nonetheless speaks her appreciation, "That's fine, that's fine. I just wanted to know. And I just want to say thank you. Thank you for taking me and the cats."

Sue and Jeanie nod to second that gratitude.

Japeth's got an awkward question of his own, "What did God look like?"

"What?" Eddie is caught off guard.

"When you talked to him." Japeth finishes, "Was he all white, big long beard?"

Eddie's face falls into memory, "He looked like my dead boss."

"Was he sort of like see-through?"

"I don't remember." Eddie, fork in hand, "I don't think so."

"That's so weird."

"Yeah," Eddie clears his throat, "Yeah, so, ah, after breakfast, I want to get those animals and food off the beddeck and down into the lower deck - it should be dry enough now."

"But what if," Sam speaks up, "what if it gets full a water again, like at night. I mean the animals will drown."

"The water outside is rising so fast," Eddie surmises, "I don't expect we'll hit any more trees."

"But there's a lot of stuff still floating around that might hit the boat." Sue finally decides to join the brainstorming.

Sue's legitimate concern, hits Eddie sidewise, like a stray limb. He almost angers, but then just as quickly, calms with a thought, "Japer, could you make me something that will warn us -- beep, like the radar thing, if the water level gets too high down there?"

Japeth, looks up from his video game, "What? Me?"

Sam parents, "And how about conserving your battery power until it stops raining."

"Yeah, we've already used up a coupla batteries in the flashlight," David reminds.

Japeth whines, "Just let me finish this game."

"Sam, could you get the short wave?" Eddie thinks out loud, "Let's see who might be still out there."

Sam finishes the last bite, rushes off to beddeck, returning with the short wave radio. Irene starts collecting the dirty plates; Eddie and Japeth set the radio up. They tune it carefully, but receive only an eerie gargling crackle. The sound of breath struggling through the red, dry esophagus of strep throat.

"There's nobody out there." David glums.

Japeth finishes his game and shuts the video toy down, "Nah… It could be just interference from the storms. I mean, I think it could be that."

"Then let's save the battery power, and not try this again 'til the sun comes out." Eddie flips the power down. The crackle abruptly disappears; the sound of a dentist's drill silenced. The crew rests a little easier without the crackle, but a lonely feeling swims in their blood. Their world has just become the exact dimensions of the ark itself.

"In that case," Japeth's the only one still in problem solving mode, "maybe I can use some wires from the short wave to make, like, some kinda water sensor for the animals. Then, uhm, when the sun comes out, I'll put the short wave back together."

Irene lowers the cages of animals down to Sam on the lower deck. Squirrels, possums, snakes, Sam stacks them carefully. David lowers the supplies down to Sam too. Japeth is on his knees with his simple sensor -- two wires stripped at the ends mounted to the wood of the ark about six inches

above the floorboards and about a quarter inch from each other. At the other end of the wires, Japeth screws his video game to the back of the pole ladder near the ceiling and hatch. A wad of tinfoil replaces one of its buttons.

Sam finishes his tasks and kneels down next to Japeth's contraption, "So, Einstein, how's this thing work?"

Japeth says nothing. Instead, he reaches down to the little remaining puddle, cups some water then drops it on the two bare wires. The video game bleeps and whistles as if he's just won a game.

"Cool!" Sam's eyes widen, he pats his brother strongly on the back. "Brilliant!"

"Cool maybe, but not really brilliant," Japeth corrects.

The bare survival essentials taken care of, the next level concerns take to voice on beddeck. Irene attempts to stop David from lowering the cougars to lower deck, "I'm telling you those cubs are not dangerous."

"Yeah, but they'll shit all over the deck." David has no intention of being calmed.

"Just as much as your little girl."

"My point exactly! Those cats are going to get hungry eventually, and Sheila isn't very quick."

Eddie's free ear catches the tone, he enters the conversation diplomatically. "Take it easy, you two. Irene, they'll be fine down there for now. You can run them around top deck whenever you want, but let's just get used to the water first and then we can get used to tigers. Okay?"

"Cougars!" Irene corrects.

"Cougar, cougars," Eddie restates, "cougars."

By evening, the crew relaxes to a game of Monopoly under the light of a couple of beddeck candles. They've decided to play teams: Sue and David, Jeanie and Sam, Irene and Eddie, Japeth alone.

"You know, Eddie," David noodles, "we must notta hit that tree before letting go a that building, I mean, we'd be sunk already."

"I know." Eddie fiddles with one of the red plastic hotels. "Plus, it was birch, and there ain't no birch in the city."

"And with the water level higher than that building, we musta drifted west and hit it in Arlington Hills."

Sam pops, "My turn!"

"Lotta birch in Arlington," Eddie remarks.

Japeth rolls the dice.

Sammer counts up the spaces in his head, "Oh yeah, Park Place, with two hotels little bro, you owe me some big bucks."

Japeth whines, "That's not fair, you guys all got partners."

"We offered to let you be on our team, but, *no*, you had to be the lone entrepreneur." Irene reminds unsympathetically.

Suddenly Jeanie starts to cry.

Sue turns caringly, "Jeanie?"

Jeanie blurts in a shockingly angry voice, "Jesus Christ, look at us! We're fucking playing Monopoly while our families are down under the ocean. What's going to be left even if we don't die?"

Jeanie's words silence the crew and halt the game. She stands up sharply in disgust. Sam's momentary enthusiasm evaporates into thin air with Jeanie's outburst. He reaches for her hand, "It's okay. It'll be okay."

Jeanie turns harsh. "No! It's not okay! Not a single house -- nothing!"

"Hey!" Sam pulls his unappreciated hand away, a bit angry as well now, "My brother's down there too! Now shut up about it; there's nothing we can do!"

Jeanie throws her monopoly money down on the board. "My parents forced God down my throat all my life and now they're dead and your dad is the Goddamned Second Coming!" She runs down to the lower deck to be with the animals.

Again the crew is silent. Their heads lower like a gang of scorned fourth graders. Their hearts drop too as the ark floats like a lone leaf in a stream with no known origin or outlet. Finally, Sam tosses his money down and gets up to follow.

Eddie lays a calm hand on Sam's knee, "Maybe she needs a bit a space, Sammer. Give her a little room."

Sam's face is expressionless, but tears silently slide out of his eyes. "It was a stupid idea to bring this game."

"Yeah, Sam. It was. We don't have to play again." Eddie folds his money, starts to collect the pieces. "Okay, let's call it a night, huh? It's been a long day. There's a whole library of books here. What do you all say we dig in?"

The group silently looks over titles, each picking something and retiring to their particular bed. There are four beds on the beddeck. Each bed hosting two people -- Japeth being the only one alone on a bed. They pull down the rolled up canvases separating and giving a little privacy to the beds.

Eddie sits alone in his area, looking at a picture of Emily he's using as a bookmark. David begins to draw the canvas to Eddie's area. Eddie quickly closes the book hiding the photo.

David whispers, "Knock knock, ah, Eddie, ah, it's been a while ... you mentioned something about bringing ... ah ... you know, condoms?"

Eddie tucks the book under his pillow, "Oh, condoms? Yeah, ask Sam about that."

"Sam?"

Eddie nods. David's eyebrow reaches for his hairline. He shrugs and bows out.

Japeth sits cross-legged on his bed with a huge astronomy picture book. Earth rotates around the sun, the third planet out, mostly blue, marble blue. Deep black space bleeds off the page. Sue sneaks her head in. "Hey Japer, how's it going?"

Japeth, a bit surprised to see Sue in his area, still keeps his nose in the book (sort of out of respect). "Pretty good, considering everything's underwater."

"Hmm, Yeah." Sue takes another step through the canvas, she's holding little Sheila asleep in her arms. "She's sleeping. Could you just watch her for little bit...maybe an hour at the most?"

Japeth closes the book on Earth and looks up sharply. "A baby? What do I do?"

"She'll sleep the whole time. Just sit here next to her, reading. If she wakes up -- we'll all hear her anyways."

"Why can't you watch her?"

Sue stiffens her lips, "Look Japeth, I haven't seen my husband in, like, a month, if you know what I mean..."

"Yeah, I know. I'm ten now," Japeth pretends to know, "I know about that stuff."

Sue lays Sheila right down next to Japer and heads out.

David peeps into Sam's area, "Sammer?"

Sam looks up from his introspective pouting. "Yeah?"

"Your dad says you brought some ... some ..." an embarrassed David is nonetheless a man on a new mission, "you know, condoms..."

"Yeah, there's about five hundred of 'em over by the powdered milk, downstairs, I mean, down below, the lower deck, whatever."

David nods awkwardly and heads down the hatch.

Up on top deck, Jeanie stands under a black umbrella, staring out over the water, the dark, misty, drizzly sky providing little comfort. Irene steps up from below carrying a book.

"Pretty crazy, huh?" Irene says in hopes of starting up a conversation."

A sad Jeanie responds, "What do you want?"

"Look," seeing that Jeanie is in no mood for a warm fuzzy girl talk, Irene gets to the newest predicament at hand. "I know it's not the best situation, and the fact is I'm terrible with words. So anyway, I'm bushed and there are two beds left ... each with a male ..."

"Are you suggesting that we share a bed?"

"I don't really care ... but I thought you might prefer it."

"Sleep wherever you like, you don't have to worry about me."

"I just thought that you and Sam..."

"Sam's a perfect gentleman. Go sleep with Mr. Johnson. That's what you want anyway."

"Hey, we're all tired. You don't have to be like that. I really was just thinking of you..."

Jeanie half concedes/half indulges in being a snotty teenager, "You're right. I'm wrong. Goodnight veterinarian lady." Jeanie climbs down the pole all the way to lower deck.

Feeling unappreciated and of little use, Irene climbs back down to beddeck. She peeps into Eddie's area. He, again, quickly closes his book.

"I guess it's you and me, Mr. Johnson." Irene says as harmlessly as possible.

Eddie takes a deep breath, "Yeah, look, it's ah, strictly business. I'm a married man."

"Strictly business?" Irene chuckles, "That mean you pay me for the services or visa versa?"

"What?..."

"I'm kidding, Eddie. Sue told me. Relax business partner ... I won't bite."

Irene scoots in uncomfortably next to him and opens her book, both of them lying face up, pretending to read.

Irene sighs, closes her book and then her eyes.

Down in the lower deck, David flashlights for the "necessary items." He catches a stare from one of the squirrels and chuckles silently at the surrealism of it all.

Jeanie steps down the pole. Respectfully, David remains silent.

"I was outta line, wasn't I?" Jeanie unexpectedly volunteers. "You all have family down there."

David stops his rummaging. The two look down at the creaking puddled wooden bottom of the boat. He takes a deep breath, puts his very important immediate mission on hold and steps over with a caring hand on Jeanie's shoulder. "Did Sam tell you how his father lost his eye?"

"Yeah?"

"I was there. I mean, I didn't do it, but I was there ripping the office open."

David's sudden openness punctures Jeanie's fragile calm and she once again begins to sob, "Why are you telling me this?"

"If Eddie can forgive me for that, nobody is gonna have a problem with you stoppin' a game of monopoly."

Jeanie tries to muffle her sobs, "Yeah, yeah, you're right."

"He's special, Jeanie, really special. We're all really special. Me, you, Samuel, this squirrel here. We are really lucky to be alive. Don't forget that."

David nods for a moment then realizes he's holding a box of condoms in his other hand. His face rushes to red as he sharply hides the box under his shirt. He awkwardly backs up the pole, whispering through an embarrassed smile, "Yep, lucky."

Irene has fallen asleep. Eddie stares intensely at the white pages of Japeth's gift - his Captain's Log. He tugs at his beard as if to pull the thoughts out onto the page. He scratches a pencil against his forehead. Rests the pencil between his ear and skull, pulls it out, replaces it nervously, finally some words break free in surprisingly elegant penmanship.

I ... ~~saw~~ I'm Eddie Johnson a carpenter. ... ~~God told me.~~ My boss got shot...Then I saw him in the kitchen....

He pauses, staring at those sentences with such intensity his teeth begin to grind. Eddie bites down on the pencil, in deadlock for several minutes.

Over the almost meditative sounds of the creaking ark, David and Sue can be heard making love -- despite their best efforts to be discreet. Irene's eyes open. Noticing that Irene has awakened, Eddie coughs awkwardly, closes the Log sharply, turns his back to Irene and hides an unexpected tear under the covers.

Jeanie and Sam are asleep in their pajamas next to each other arm in arm -- like teenagers at the movies. They, too, wake with the sounds of David and Sue. Embarrassed to even look at each other over the moans, they stare up at the close ceiling. After a few minutes Jeanie rolls over and kisses Sam on the cheek. He smiles, they make out for a few minutes, then snuggle until they fall asleep again.

On the other side of the canvas, those sounds prompt Japeth to put his Wright brothers book down, "I knew it!" Japeth mumbles to himself, "I watch cable movies too!"

Then toward the sleeping baby he says, "Your mom and your dad, Sammy and Jeanie, my dad and that animal doctor." Then in a rather dodgy Humphrey Bogart voice, "In, like, twenty years, looks like it's you and me ... kid."

Day 24

Sam carves the 10th "X" on the railing's etched calendar; he looks up into the dusty gray skies over the hood of his raincoat and shakes his head at the relentless storm. The ark bobbles alone in a sea of rainwater, miles upon miles of water.

Eddie ambles over to David, "Come down to the lower deck with me."

David follows unquestioningly. The two stand face to face. Eddie takes a deep breath, and runs his hand through his beard. "Uh, look," he pulls out the Captain's Log, "Japeth gave this to me. It's for journaling. It's a good idea, it's just that I ain't much of a writer. I tried. I tried, but the words don't come."

"Writer's block."

Eddie snorts through a grin, "No." He pats David on the shoulder and hands the journal over to him, "This Captain's Log is now the First Mate's Log."

"Eddie, I ain't no writer neither."

"Write in the book -- and that's an order."

"But Eddie…"

"That is, unless Sue is too much of a distraction for you."

David falls speechless for a second, "Oh, I'm sorry about that. We hadn't been ... it was a long time, Eddie. We tried to be quiet."

Eddie smiles. "Yeah, I know big guy. Just use the condoms; we ain't gonna be birthing no babies at sea." He pulls a pencil from behind his ear, taps the journal twice and hands the pencil to David, "and write in the book."

Day 29

Japeth slips over into Sam's room. "Watchya reading?"

Sam mumbles uncaringly, "Some dumb book."

"Do you thinka Henry ever?"

Sam hides an unwelcome tug at his heart, masking that emotion with disinterest, "Yeah."

"You think he's okay?"

Still dishonestly calm, "Yeah."

"You don't seem like you think he's okay."

Sam closes the book impatiently. "Japer, yes, I wonder about him. I worry about him. Is that better?"

"I didn't mean for you to get mad."

"I'm not mad. I'm not mad. Okay?"

Japeth stands silent at the door, "Never mind."

Sam lets out a long breath of air, "Yes Japer, you know, I do worry for him. He could be so mean to you

sometimes. I mean before he went to junior high and when you were just a baby, he'd play with me a lot more. He was a lot more fun before he went to junior high, before he got all serious … before mom died."

Japeth stares out the porthole, "Do you miss mom?"

"Yes, I miss her, too. But I'm sort of used to that. Henry? I'm not used to missing him."

"Maybe he got with the Jagulskis like dad said."

"Yeah, maybe."

Japeth lies down on the mat next to Sam. "I think I miss Henry the way you miss mom."

Finishing up a lovely meal of canned ravioli right out of the can, Japeth marks another X on the calendar -- the 20th.

David digs the remaining spaghetti sauce from the bottom of the can. "It's Monday again, isn't it Japer?"

"Seems like it's Monday every seven days or so." Irene jokes.

Sam and Jeanie smile politely at that while Japeth pulls out a DVD and sets up the laptop.

"So, Japer, what's this week's Monday Night Movie?" Irene continues.

Japeth, in his best T2 voice, "I'll be back."

Jeanie groans, "Oh, no, not another Arnold movie."

"...In digital surround ... " Japeth pops out of his character voice, "but you'll just have to imagine that," he quips and starts up the movie.

Everyone descends to beddeck, situating themselves to get a better view around the little laptop -- it's light giving an out-of-place bluish techno-luminescence to the cabin.

Irene pulls David to the side before joining the group. "David?"

"Irene?" David's a little surprised to be pulled aside by Irene.

"Eddie's wife…," Irene starts, "… what happened to her?"

"Wow, yeah, well I, uh, I never met her, but he carries that picture of her around all the time. Joe said she died giving birth. I never asked Eddie about it."

"He must've really loved her."

"Yep."

Irene takes a deep somber breath, "Well, that's so sad. Thanks for telling me."

"Sure, uhm," David scratches uncomfortably at the back of his neck. Now, he's got a question for Irene, "Uhm, Eddie gave me this diary, ah, journal thing, not that I wanta, I don't really, but Eddie gave it to me so, I'm gonna give it a go… anyway, I have no idea… no idea what ta write. I've been staring at it for a week, and anyway, Sue said that you scientific types .."

"…We keep journals?"

"Yeah…do you?"

Irene smiles, sighing a segue to this new topic, "So you want some advice on how to get started on it?"

"That's exactly it."

"Oh, well yes, we scientific types do keep journals -- not sure how fascinating they are, but … basically, we just record what we're experiencing -- name, date, subject at hand. However, you can start with just what you said about not feeling so comfortable with the idea."

"Yeah?"

"Yeah. I didn't really like documenting at first, now I don't really think about it, it's part of the process. It's quite useful to look back and read, because the memory is a funny thing -- not a good place to put important information."

"Wow, thanks. I'll see what I can do."

"You go, Thoreau, and thanks again for the scoop on Eddie. I didn't know."

David scrunches his lips and nods his head, "Yep."

Eddie grunts at Japeth's movie. He gets up, hobbles silently to the shelves and runs his fingers across the books. His index finger hesitates on the Bible. He taps it while scratching his beard. A quick glance along the other shelf; he yanks out a different title all together -- "Giving Birth at Home."

While the rest enjoy the small screen film, Eddie reads the how-to manual concerning the greatest of home projects. Eventually, his eyelids grow heavy; he pulls out his picture of Emily and falls asleep with it in his hand.

After the movie, Irene crawls into bed. She looks over to Eddie who has the book on giving birth in one hand and Emily in the other. The tragic irony brings some unexpected water to her eyes. She gently takes the book out of his hand and sets it off the bed. She delicately pulls the photo from between his big callused fingers and slides it into his shirt pocket. Then with a sympathetic sigh, she gives Edward Johnson an appreciative kiss on the forehead and snuggles in next to him.

So I'm David MacMay. Eddie gave me this ~~diary~~ thing. Journal thing. I aint written anything since high school, I hated writing ~~shit~~ stuff. Anyway, its not like theres alot to do on the boat, now that we cleared the rooftops. Just rocking. I'm so glad Sue's here, Sue and Sheila. Sue and Sheila. Dam, when I turned my head tward the boat and saw them. I just

about died. I just about died right there. Sue and Sheila here with me. Its amaizing, its really all been amaizing. Not real. The flood, the ark. Me. All not real. And now my family.

Day 35

Well, I'm alive. I'm in a boat. Me and Eddie bilt it. A lot of hammering. We're floating. We've been floating a while. Sammers keeping the days in x marks. We got animals. Shit if it didn't rain like Eddie said. It's all because Eddie talked to God. Anyway. We're floating and it's raining. It's like raining a real lot. I'd say cats and dogs, but that'd remind me too much of the smell in lower deck. Just a lot of rain. Almost can't remember when it wasn't raining. Nothing is dry. Everything is damp. Even my bones.

Day 36

I'm so happy to see Sheila and sue. I ~~thought~~ I think alot of people on this boat are angry or scared or upset. I know Sue is scared. And that Sam's girlfriend, she really misses her family. I can understand that! But, me. But I feel so happy. Happy Grateful, lucky. . I am soooo lucky. I almost feel guilty for feeling this lucky, while they aren't feeling so good. And it's so dark and wet out. But, Privilegd. I don't

remember. Wait, besides sue marrying me... I don't remember ever feeling privilegd, and Sue... well, she had to marry me. Not sure I should write that down. I mean, I loved her. I still do, but Sheila.. she just didn't ask.

Day 37

I can't believe this thing actually floats, I mean, I just kept hammering nails into it, some wood glue and alot of just listening to Eddie, or more watching than listening. He's like doubled what he used to say, I mean before the whole God thing. But still doesn't have much to say. Even at double.

Anyway, I put alot of nails into that dam hull and I'm frankly amaized water isn't bustin through. And there's water coming at us from all directions. That branch gave us all a scare.. but I don't know, just being there next to Eddie...I wasn't a scared of nothing. Just kept workin on it as if I knew, completely knew that we'd get it fixed. Shit, Eddie Johnson's ark. This is Eddie Johnson's ark. Eddie is the ark.

It's sort of undescribable that feeling of being trusted, wanted, believed in. Eddie comin to pick me up that day. Shit. All my life, I just did what I needed to get by. I didn't even notice Eddie being good to people. He never made a scene about it, and me, ... takin care of number one. Then I go banging

eddies eye out. Why is it that the good guys always take the whack in the head? I didn't do it actually. Joe did. But, as much as I tell myself I didn't do it. I know, I absolutely know, if I had half the balls of Eddie, I coulda stopped Joe from doin it.

Geeze, look at me. I never wrote this much even in school.

Day 39

In the middle of the night, Japeth cracks one eye open. All are asleep, the now worn boat creaking in an almost uncanny rhythm with Eddie's snoring. But something is different. Something is missing. Japeth holds his breath and listens with all his ear might. Both eyes are open now and scanning the beddeck. They finally stop on a porthole. Japeth releases his held breath through a smile, he slips on his socks and scurries over to Eddie's area. He whispers over his father, "Dad! Dad! The rain..."

Irene, with even a softer whisper, "Sshhh. He's sleeping."

Japeth softens his speech, "But the rain stopped."

"Really?" Irene whispers back, "Let's have a look."

"You and me?"

Irene nods.

Irene and Japeth stand on deck holding hands. Huge rolling clouds drift in slow motion. Gray and black, the clouds float like curtains over their heads. A light breeze picks up and a part between two dark clouds widens revealing a sliver of deep marble ebony and blue sky.

Japeth points. As if in answer, a star peeks through the parting clouds. Irene smiles. As if in answer, the river of blueblack sky opens even wider, staging a glittering cast of shimmering silver stars.

"I forgot what they looked like. They're so, so beautiful, Japer, aren't they?"

"I didn't forget."

"Look at that one, that bright one. Isn't that gorgeous?"

"That one's not a star."

"It's not?"

That's Jupiter. It's a planet."

"Well, I know Jupiter is a planet, but I didn't know ... well, really, that's Jupiter?"

"You wanna see Saturn?"

Irene takes her eyes off the sky for a minute to shine a smile down to this bright small boy, "Sure."

The clouds speed to the edges of the dim horizon/stage.

"Over there by the Big Dipper. You see it. It's kinda red."

"Look at that, Japer. Planets. I never stopped to look at planets."

"Well, Earth is one too."

"That's right."

"Isn't that amazing?"

"It's not that late, huh?" Japeth looks down at his watchless wrist. "Maybe like 11 o'clock."

"I guess. Something like that."

"The dipper hasn't shifted much."

"What does that mean?"

"We haven't drifted too far. I mean, we're not over Africa or something like that."

Irene, takes a deep introspective breath, "We're not over Africa." She repeats as if the repetition will make that observation seem normal. She looks out over all the water.

Japeth joins her in a far away gaze, "Nope."

"Hey little man, come on, let's go back to bed. We can let the others sleep."

"Sleep? Let's wake everyone up!"

"Shhhhh. You know what, this could mean a lot of work for tomorrow. Let's let them sleep. Why don't we bring up the cougars and you can play with them a while if you can't sleep."

Pinpoint-sharp beams blister through the widening cracks between planks -- blades of sunlight pierce. As the little boat slowly drifts in a lazy whirlpool, the intense white rays slide across the sleeping sailors: Eddie and Irene, Japeth with a cougar cub cuddled under each arm, David and family, Sam and Jeanie holding hands in their sleep. The shard of light paints a brilliant glowing orange band across their beds, then their heads until it finally burns through David's eyelids, evaporating his slumber. He rubs the sleep out of his smiling green eyes fixed on the porthole. Sunlight floods through like water from a fire hose. The boat turns further. The light, searching out the youngest heart aboard, finds Sheila; floating lint dancing in the beams, the mustard-orange tickles her chin until she chuckles in her sleep. It plays with the child, working her chuckles up into a butterfly swarm of giggles that flutter about beddeck waking the last tired stormtrooper.

David gets up first, effortlessly ascending the pole with excitement. The rest follow without pause.

Up on deck, David pokes his finger at the sun, stumbling on his laughter and on his first sentence of the very new day. "You know, I half expected to see JJ's freakin' grin on that thing."

Eddie smiles peacefully, shakes his head in disbelief. Without a word he goes back down for the supplies on the lower deck. David having already said more words than necessary, the rest squint their eyes at the sun, silently absorbing its warmth with their cheeks. Hands in terry cloth pockets, feet in socks and soggy slippers, they stand on the fiery edge of light, each beaming like a birthday child in front of a well frosted cake blazing with burning candles, flames reflecting in their eyes.

Eddie returns with the solar panels. He places them on top of the garage, then turns to Japeth. "Japeth, get that short wave back together for me. Will ya?"

Eddie's voice takes a second to register, Japeth's delayed attention kicks in, breaking his trance. "Oh, Oh yeah." He hops down the pole trading with Eddie a chance at the solar hypnotism.

The group reprises its meditative state.

Too soon, Japeth pops back up with the radio and some bad news. "Dad? Uhm."

Sam turns away from the sun with an air of skepticism. "Great Einstein! You can't put it back together?"

Japeth counters, "It's not that."

"What is it, son?" Eddie asks.

"Bugs."

Sam sneers, "Bugs?"

"Bugs?" David queries, "Like computer bugs?"

"No," Japeth explains, "well, sort of. I mean they call computer bugs, bugs, because a long time ago, they really were bugs."

Jeanie's shoulders rise and tighten. "Are you saying we got bugs on the boat?"

"I'm saying, bugs got into this thing. Then when I turned it on just now ... they fried it." Japeth shakes the electronic box and a few dead bugs fall out. Jeanie shrieks.

"Did you put the wires back in?" Sam interrogates.

"I only used the wires from the microphone. That wouldn't make any difference."

"Maybe you should put them back anyways and then try it." Sam continues his line.

Japeth simply shakes his head.

Eddie finally closes his dropped jaw, "Well, can you fix it? I mean whatever the bugs broke."

"You guys might think I'm a genius, but you didn't grow up with computers. I'm just a hack. I don't know anything about transistors or circuit boards."

David encourages, "What about that sensor thing you made?"

"That's a simple switch. It's nothing. I didn't even touch the circuit board."

"It's okay son." Eddie consoles, "We'll have more battery power for another movie. In the mean time, I'd like you to just take a look at it. Scrape off the bugs or whatever."

"Not another Arnold film!" Jeanie shrugs.

"I second that," Sue concurs.

Irene sighs, "So, then, I guess we just float around until all this evaporates? Or ... uhm... falls off the planet?"

Eddie takes a deep breath and tosses his hands up as if to say, "I don't know!"

"Or freezes," Sam offers.

David turns his attention to Sam, "Freezes?"

"Yeah, the news was saying that the glaciers were melting," Sam continues.

"Maybe that's why the water rose so fast," David noodles.

"So maybe they'll freeze again?" Sam finishes his thought.

Everyone turns their wondering eyes toward Eddie, but he still doesn't know. Irene studies the fallen insects.

Not burdened by his crew's expectations, Eddie attends more concrete matters, "Check out the other equipment, Japeth."

"Blatteria." Irene finally blurts, nose down over the radio's droppings.

"What?" David replies.

"Cockroach larvae," Doc Irene clarifies, "We got roaches."

Jeanie grits her teeth, "I hate roaches."

"If we set the iguana's free," Irene suggests, "they'll eat the roaches."

"Did I say I liked iguanas?" Jeanie's sarcasm resurfaces.

"You were right about the cougars," David's parental instincts kick in, "they've been very good around Sheila, but what about the lizards, will they bite her?

Japeth jokes, "Not if there's enough roaches."

Irene runs her hand through the hair on Japeth's head and says, "They shouldn't. They're timid and stay away from people by nature, but we'll just have to watch 'em. And if they bite, then we'll just have to use a bandage."

"How about mating?" Eddie chimes in, "I don't know how long we'll be floating. Are we prepared to have little iguanas all over the place?"

"They're both males, Eddie. Sorry," Irene responds.

Sam turns his head to Eddie, "Sorry, Dad, we just grabbed what we could."

Eddie chuckles, "Great, a busted short wave radio and two boy iguanas!"

"And lots of cockroaches," Sue nudges.

The stymied crew pauses over the newest problems, then Irene reminds, "But it did stop raining."

"Yeah, and everything else looks like it's working. I mean it turns on and lights up." Japeth shows off the other equipment.

The crew lightens up too, nods and relaxes a bit under the sun.

Eddie tends to the business of staying alive, "How can we make sure the roaches won't bust our other equipment?"

"Do we have any raid? Or poison?" Sue asks.

David shakes his head.

Irene narrows her eyes, "We better not, I got two mischievous kittens here."

"Two words." Japeth says, "Duct tape."

"Tape?" Sammy asks.

"Nail the duct tape upside down like around the equipment. If roaches try to walk over, they'll get stuck." Japeth expands his two words into two sentences.

"And become boy iguana food." Sam concludes.

Eddie rocks his head back and forth in agreement, "Okay, Sam, why don't you do that? The tape is in my toolbox. Japeth, get the radar going and depth sounder. I wanna know how far down there everything is."

The boys say in unison, "Aye, aye, sir," then head down to the lower decks.

David stares into the sun, "You think it'll start up again?"

Eddie, still thinking of the roaches, "What?"

David, still staring up, "The rain."

Of course Eddie still doesn't know the answer. And once again the crew stands in silence.

Jeanie's answer breaks that silence, "No."

David turns his attention to this hardheaded teenager, "How can you be so sure?"

"Forty days and forty nights." Jeanie digs her fingers into the carved X's, "twenty-six X's plus, like two weeks before we've been floating, that's how long it's been raining."

"So?" David's not catching on.

Sue clears her throat, "David went to public school." Then she fills in the blanks to David. "forty days and forty nights -- everything in the Bible happens for forty days and forty nights."

Day 42

It stopped raining. That's amaizing. I can't believe it. I just thought it would rain for the rest of my life. But it stopped. Today. I forgot what the sun looked like. I swear I thought it gave up on us.

We've been out here, out here... I guess I could say ... at sea for a couple a weeks or so, One of Eddie's kids is marking them, counting them, but it really doesn't matter to me. I mean, I think they're all waiting, angshus to land this thing... sometimes I can see Sue or the vet lady gazing out over the horizon scanning for land, or an answer, or something. They're all sort of angshus. I knew ~~can~~ I know with Eddie around they feel calmer, even when he doesn't feel calm. He's like an anchor to their worries. But its funny, he seemed so calm to me before, I mean I worked with the guy for a year, I never saw him upset, or cry or...even frustrated, but out here, I feel like the ~~so~~ storm or the flood, or the sea, its

more is inside him than out there. We're just floating in this boat right on the waves of Eddie. Yeah, so they're all a little worried, angshus to land. But me. My whole life is, I've been out bobbling around in the waves like Sheila's little boat in the bath. Now, I feel, I feel like I'm on solid ground. For the first time in my life I finally feel like I have a purpose. I don't know why, but Eddie gave me a second chance and that is worth more than my whole life before sue. I don't plan on fucking that up. It's good to wake up. Even in this boat, even floating in this uncertainty. It's good to wake up and know your mission. Check the bottom deck, make sure know what is creaking, clear out the shit for the stalls, cook if its my turn, clean the dishes if its my turn, be ever ready ever ready to do whatever Eddie thinks need to be done. I used to just float in my daydreams, or float on no thoughts at all, I don't know, make it from Monday to Friday just on thoughts of the weekend. That's funny, lots of guys dream of fishing on a boat, look at me, I get up every morning and I'm on a boat. My life is this boat. This boat, sue and Sheila.

Day 44

The group enjoys a delicious sunset as Eddie's sons set the table for another dinner up in the garage. Irene opens the garage door, setting the cans on the counter.

"Ravioli again!" Sue feigns joy.

"What?" Irene replies. "It was the closest stuff to the hatch."

"I'm joking -- really," Sue finishes, "I used to love ravioli."

"How about caviar and swordfish?" Irene jests.

An idea pops into Sam's head, "I don't know about caviar, but why don't we go fishing tomorrow morning!"

Japeth speaks with his mouth full of ravioli, "You can use roaches for bait."

"You know how to fish David?" Sam asks.

David looks over at Sue with his reply, "No, I went to public school."

Without ever entering it, Eddie leaves the conversation. He takes his can of grub and walks to the back of the boat to watch the sunset. Japeth quietly follows.

Like a dish of molten steel, the sun dips into the long sleepy blue horizon. Swallowed whole, cooled by the infinity of the sea, the skies cool too.

After standing peacefully for a few moments, Japeth speaks. "I'm sorry Dad, about the radio."

"Don't worry Japer, you did good. You did real good."

"And the sounder, I think it's working perfect, it's just we're too high. I'll read the manual again tomorrow."

"Really, Japer, You're doing great."

"Then why don't I feel so great?"

Japer's uncharacteristically sad tone pulls Eddie down to one knee. He looks Japer right in the eye. "I love you

Japer. I'm so proud of you; your mother would have been so proud of you."

"I know, but what about Henry? What about Henry, Dad? Would he be proud of me?"

Eddie puts down the can and hugs his youngest son strongly. Japer hugs back; both break into tears. "Yes, Japer, Henry would've been proud of you. Both your mother and Henry would've been proud of you."

Day 47

I'm thinking about that day Jeanie lost it. She got real pissed off. But I think she just said what we all were thinking. We were all thinking it, but we didn't want to say it. I know I didn't. I still don't want to think about it. But it's like something we submurge inside ourselves. It stays down for a while, but every once in a while it comes up into our conshusness. I mean here we are on this boat, the boat God told Eddie to bild. I guess, we just all believe him. We just believe him that its like God said and the world needs to be cleansed. So that we just guess that means everybody dies. That doesn't make much sense to me, I'm not saying there aren't lots of people that don't deserve it. I bet there alot that do. But all of them except us? And me? I don't feel like I deserve not to be drowned. I don't know about Irene or Eddie's kids, they don't even talk about that. In fact, it sort of scary to me just to write about it. I mean, it's funny, I

didn't care about to many people before, the flood. You know, just me and then my family. But now, here I am caring about people I don't even know and getting this sick feeling in my stomach whenever I think about them down there. I think the others on the boat feel that sick feeling too. So we try our best not to think about it and we defenitly never talk about it. That's why Jeanie's little explosion that day, no body got mad at her. She's right. But we got no idea what to do about it, just believe in Eddie and keep the ark floating.

Day 49

Twilight at sea. Irene emerges halfway through the hatch on the deck, scanning 360 degrees. She finishes the climb up and notices an open can of red paint on the stern railing and a rope over the edge. She tilts her head in wonder and slowly approaches the paint can. A hand pops up from behind the railing and startles her. She stops mid-step, wide-eyed, a gasp. The hand innocently grabs the can, disappears, then reappears to return the can to the railing. Irene cautiously steps closer. She tentatively peeks over the railing from port side to see Eddie, saddled in the rope and hanging out over the back of the boat, painting.

Surprised, then suddenly feeling as though she's trespassing on his privacy, she backs away slowly, bringing up the collar of a T-shirt she'd borrowed from him to cover her throat.

By the time she returns to beddeck, Sue and Sheila have already fallen asleep and Japeth is shutting down the mini-theater. "You missed it."

Irene quips, "Let me guess -- he saves the day."

"How'd you know?" Japeth pops.

"Lucky guess." Irene mumbles. "Anyway, I'm tired and I've got to pee."

"David's in there," Japeth refers to the bathroom.

"Great, I'll wait… Couldn't your father have built an ark with two and half baths?"

Japeth shrugs.

David slips out of the toilet. "You looking for a seat with a hole in it?"

"Yep." Irene grabs a book off the shelf and stumbles in.

"That was good, but I like the second one better," David says to Japeth.

"Really?" Japeth tucks away the DVD, checks the laptop's battery power levels, then plops himself down on his bed to sleep.

Irene comes out of the bathroom to find everyone asleep -- even Eddie. She looks down at the book, realizing she'd read nearly fifty pages while on the commode. She chuckles at herself, drops Eddie a compassionate glimpse, but her curiosity overcomes her and she climbs back up to deck. This time leaning as far as she can over the stern railing, what Eddie has painted in red is easily legible, though upside down to her. The name "Emily" extends across the back of Eddie Johnson's ark.

Day 50

The sun was bouncing off the waves today. It's so good to see the sun. My world has become so small. Just the boat, these six people and Sheila. Used to be a lot of rain too, but now

it's just the whole planet is blue, blue water, blue sky and this rickity piece of crap boat that Eddie and I bilt from a lumberyard in Columbus Ohio. Columbus, the name of our city-- isn't that a kick? God's gotta have some sense of humor.

Day 51

Another day on the boat, surprise, nothing much of interest today, Sheila stared at me for the longest time. Like five minutes without looking away. SO I didn't either, like she and I were the only two on this boat. The bed mats have finally dried out. I'm so lucky to have her, I'm doubly lucky to have her respect ... I think if we were still in Columbus, Sheila staring at me all serious ls like that... I think I woulda had to look away.

Day 53

An iguana munches on a slow roach; Sammy nudges it off the railing so that he can make the 39th X. Jeanie plays with the cougars, now nearly twice the size of when they boarded. The rest dig into lunch up on deck: canned corn and beef jerky.

Down in the lower deck, Eddie rummages for some dessert. A parakeet pokes through its cage at Eddie's hand. Eddie pulls his hand back fast. "Oh, yer a quick one,

aren'tchya?" he says to the parakeet. The bird doesn't reply. But Eddie smiles in thought, a certain playful smile that hasn't been on his face since he was a kid, certainly not since Emily died. He looks into the cage, into the bird's mirror; he winks his one good eye at himself and giggles like a child.

Up on deck, David bangs his empty can of corn on the table and yells facetiously down the hatch, "Hey Eddie, where's my dessert? I'm a hungry man!"

Eddie pops his head out of the hatch with a parakeet on his shoulder, laughing. "Aye, matey, shut yer trap, louse, you're lucky I feedya atall!"

Stunned, shocked into absolute quiet by Eddie's playfulness and of course, the incredible insanity of Eddie Johnson, patch on one eye, blazingly yellow and red bird on one shoulder, a bent spoon in the opposite hand, joking like a drunken pirate, the hush lasts a long second before all aboard burst into laughter.

Eddie came up on deck to day with one of Irene's bird's on his shoulder, with that dam patched eye -- that was the biggest laugh I had since it started raining. The biggest laugh I think we all had. I couldn't believe it. Eddie Johnson -- I don't remember ever seeing him joke. And then there he is with the friggin parrot. I swear to God, it was the first time I could look him in the face without the site of that patch slapping me with a lump of gilt in the stomach. I done alot of stupid things in my life, but that patch tops the list.

Day 56

David and Eddie lean back on a couple of crates, their lines cast. They squint their eyes out into the distance, waiting for a bite. Sam etches the 42nd X in the railing.

Day 57

Seems like everybodys kind of taken on Eddie's way, I mean, like we all had ideas before the water got high, but after you see the rooftops of your town disappear, you pretty much just eksept that Eddie was right. I'm not sure I mean like believe, I just mean eksept. Your town underwater, that'll shut up even the biggest mouth. I mean, dam, even bill, bill was going to steamroll over Eddie, but even he had his tail between his legs. Anyway, we all don't have a whole lot to say, we just took on Eddie's way. That's sort of weird, but I think it's sort of calm. I used to run my mouth, not a thought of what I was saying more than a second. I used to be so full of shit. But a town full of water.. kind of washes the shit out of you. I wonder what made Eddie quiet so long ago. Maybe it was Emily passing. I didn't know him before Emily, maybe he ran his mouth too. My head was hard. I needed Eddie to come pick me up that day. I probably needed the flood too. I don't know if I would have wised up any other way. I wish I didn't

need to do something really stupid like not stop Eddie from getting whacked. It's almost like my mistake caused this whole flood. Like God is up there looking down from the blue sky, nothing to get in his way of seeing all the crap we're doing down here -- I mean, the skys were so blue for the longest I've ever seen. Not a cloud. So maybe like just when he'd had about all he could watch, I go and let Joe knock Eddie's eye out. I could have so easily not done that. What was I thinking? I was so stupid. That's just it, I wasn't thinking. Anyway. Anyway, we're just not talking much on this boat. Just keeping it floatin.

Day 63

　　　Eddie is at his Japeth's bed, petting his son's sweating head with a cool damp cloth. Japeth's head rolls on a seemingly rubber neck, his breaths uneven and fast, cheeks puffing occasionally with the threat of another heave. Though he's awake, his eyes are more than half closed with exhaustion and weakness. Eddie stares hard at Japeth, as if great concentration might be enough to cure him of whatever sickness swims in his blood. Pouring salt in an open wound, the faint sound of Japeth's video game whistles in Eddie's head.

　　　David sticks his face up out of the lower deck hatch.

　　　Eddie throws an annoyed eyebrow at David, "Shhh. He's almost sleeping again." Then in an agitated whisper, "And where the hell is that goddamned game of his? It's driving me crazy."

David, taut lipped, pauses to allow Eddie a few seconds to calm.

Eddie exhales through his nose. He can see bad news on David's face. "Jesus, David, what is it?"

"That birch, you know that branch? Well it broke through the hole. That's why Japeth's game is going crazy."

Eddie shakes his head and feels Japeth's forehead.

David mutters, "I can't stop the leaking; it's all like wet cardboard."

Irene overhears and peeks in. "Look, I'll watch Japeth, you guys get the coffee grinder routine going."

Hiding gritted teeth behind his lips, Eddie kisses Japer, and shuffles off. David rounds up Jeanie, Sam and Sue to start the bucket dumping and manual pump (coffee grinder). Up on deck, Eddie's running the pump. Jeanie is the last of the chain of bucket carriers, up on top deck too, dumping the water over the edge. She and Eddie are the only two on upper deck. Eddie is lost in worry, glossy-eyed, looking very worn by now, and troubled. Jeanie silently tosses bucket after bucket as they're handed to her; she looks listlessly over at him. Just then, out of the west, a huge rainbow blazes.

Having spent many, many days in Sunday school, Jeanie recites in rote, "And God said, 'I have set my rainbow in the clouds. It will be the sign of the covenant I am making between me and you and every living creature: Never again will the waters become a flood to destroy all life. Never again shall I curse the earth because of man. And never again shall I cut off all life as I have done.'"

Eddie snaps his head up harshly. He snarls, "Is that from the Bible? I mean word for word?"

Jeanie, somewhat intimidated by Eddie's tone, "Uhm, pretty much ... my parents ..."

"What verse?" Eddie interrupts.

Jeanie pauses.

"What damn verse!?" Eddie insists.

"Genesis, six or seven or something like that."

Without another word, Eddie runs down the pole against the bucket train. He tears the Bible from the shelf, rips through the pages for the verse, as if he were rummaging through hairs on the heads of his sons for lice. He finds what he's looking for and lunges back to deck. Stepping without hesitation to the railing, he hurls the Holy Bible at the rainbow. The pages flutter and twist toward the sky, the book peaks then falls into the sea, breaking the surface of the water with a splash, and is gone.

Jeanie, afraid, steps back holding her mouth shut.

Screaming mad, Eddie howls, "You promised you wouldn't do it again! You promised you wouldn't! All those people! You are not a good God!!! You are a murderer!" He points down into the depths. "Just as bad as they were!"

The pale white sun looks down at Eddie's pointed finger and the little ark bobbing in the waves, a mere speck in the breadth of oceans curving with the sphere of the earth. A few scattered clouds round out a planet frosted with billions upon billions of gallons of rainwater.

Eddie's curses are answered with some sputtering static from the radio, but nothing else.

A distraught Sam rushes up on deck. "Dad? Japeth is vomiting again. I don't know what ta do."

"I don't know either!" Eddie kicks the radio and stomps down into the ship to see Japeth. Working himself into a fury he rips the canvas open into Japeth's area and then is suddenly, wholly and completely stopped in his tracks to see the old dirty homeless, window-washing man from ramp 242 Columbus sitting on Japeth's bed. The man calmly applies the damp cloth to Japeth's head. Japeth has fallen back to sleep, a bucket of fresh vomit just off to the side of the bed.

His hair wiry and dirt gray, his beard mangy and long, his face wrinkled like a cabbage patch doll, a very little man, he begins to speak. "Nice ark Eddie. Beautiful, really. Mine, I had to build to specs. That's how He was back then. Build it to specs." The old man looks over the cabin. "This one is just as much yours as his. More yours, even. He's always wanted things that way. It's just, well, you know, things get crazy. People can't even trust each other, you can imagine God would get a bit shy. Start to use the stiff ruler, fire and brimstone. But this is a nice ark. Very creative. I would have been proud to sail this one."

Eddie is halted by the appearance of this man on his ark, but still very comfortable swimming in his own problems, "Yeah well, there's a hole in the lower deck leakin' like a son of a bitch. We can't stop it this time. In a couple a hours we'll be under."

The old man, unimpressed, "Uh-huh, we had problems with ours too. We lost all hope, too. Ham caught pneumonia; we thought we'd lose him. Me, I got some fungus on my feet that almost crippled me. And believe me, we had a lot more water in ours and I had a lot more animals and no veterinarian lady."

Sam pops his head as he passes by. "Oh, good, he stopped. I was really scared there." Then he takes off without mention of the old man.

Eddie watches Sam leave and is confused that Sam failed to notice the old man. Eddie turns a calmer head to the old man. He whispers, "So how'd ya manage? How'd ya fix a leak like ours? Patches won't hold anymore."

"And the wood is soaked and wretched. I know. I know. It's not our fault. It was our first boat. We couldn't have thought of everything."

"So how'd ya fix it? How'd ya manage?"

"We didn't fix it. But we managed. Faith, I suppose. Something always happened. Something always happened to keep us afloat."

The bucket train continues; no one sees the old man but Eddie. David pops his head from the lower hatch with another bucket full of water. "Eddie, we can't keep this up all day. What are we gonna do?"

Eddie looks at David without a response then turns back to the old man. "So that's it? You can't fix my ship?"

David looks up at Eddie, baffled. "Well, I mean ... hey, what's with you? We're all working... I could kinda use another hand down here." Concerned and a tad confused, David squints toward Eddie, then at Japeth sleeping. No time to figure it out, he returns to the task at hand.

The old man answers. "I wasn't sent to fix your ship Eddie. My duties to sailing are long over. I never boarded another vessel since. Even now I'm admiring your work, but I'd be happier off this thing. This one's yours Eddie."

"But he lied! He broke his promise! Never again a flood, never again killing all life!"

"Don't be so quick to judge, Eddie."

"But a man's word is his honor. How can I respect a broken promise like this? All those people? Henry? Jeanie's whole family?"

"Uh-huh, Eddie, it's not just the people this time. It's the whole ball of wax. The planet was dried up and cracking. You guys had a hole in the ozone the size of the Red Sea. ... It just needed rain. It needed to be cleansed and..." the old man struggles for a word, "... recycled."

"Recycled?" Eddie drops his jaw. "I don't give a damn the circumstances! If he couldn't know the future, he shouldn't have made the goddamn promise! A man's word is his honor. How could *you* let it go? His covenant was with *you*!"

"Relax. He is still a good God and you still don't see the whole picture."

"I read the verses! I saw the rainbow! Don't you remember? He promised it to you!"

"Yeah, yeah, uh-huh, the verses. Yeah, the verses - they got the gist."

"The gist!?" Eddie's eyes redden.

The old man takes a deep breath and looks down at his folded hands, "Yep, the gist."

Eddie's red eyes further narrow, "So there was no covenant?'"

"There was. There was. But it wasn't with me. It was with all of us. I was just the one there to shake His hand."

Boom! A huge sound, the sound of one thousand bombs rumbles through the ark. Eddie reaches for the ceiling to steady himself as a few loose nails rattle free with the low frequency vibrations.

"Mr. Johnson!!! Mr. Johnson???" Jeanie yells down the hatch, "A plane!"

Eddie looks up the hatch, then back at the old man, but the man is gone. Instead, Japeth starts to vomit again. Sam slides in off the chain to catch Japeth's newest upchuck with an empty bucket. Eddie shakes his head. Walking up the rungs slowly, he mumbles, "Can't be. They fell out of the sky weeks ago."

Eddie gets on deck just in time to see the plane rapidly approach. "My God, my God, it *is* a plane."

Jeanie's voice trembles, "But it's flying in way too fast."

The white aircraft nears the water with incredible speed.

Eddie's mutter is barely audible, "It's not flying ... *it's falling.*"

The huge white flyer, fat in the middle, stubby wings, nose pointed almost straight down, sharply levels to the

surface of the water. Horizontal and still moving fast across the horizon, the tips of the waves battering its wings, it pulls up, porpoises, one hundred yards, slowing with its ascent and then seemingly stops, frozen, before tipping back downward again. Nose first, the craft splashes into the ocean making a dramatic spectacle of itself. It submerges immediately and completely, leaving the ocean and ark so unchanged, Eddie and Jeanie begin to wonder if it really happened at all.

Sue in beddeck, holding a bucket full of water up over her head, waits for Jeanie to take it from her through the hatch. But Jeanie's completely distracted, so Sue climbs up and dumps it over the railing herself. "What's with you two?" Sue grumbles, somewhat annoyed by their lack of participation, "and what the heck was that sound?"

Sam steps up to toss the bucket of Japeth's puke. He turns to look wherever it is that Jeanie and Eddie are looking.

Then reprising its magnificent spectacle, the craft re-emerges on the other side of the ark. The four on board turn 180 degrees to see. Like a great dolphin, it shoots up out of the water ten or twenty yards high, levels, then belly flops to a floating stop.

Jeanie, Sue, Eddie, and Sam on the deck of the ark, stand dumfounded, jaws wide.

Sue drops the empty bucket, "What is that?"

"That don't look like no plane," Sam mumbles.

"Keep bailing!" Eddie comes to his senses.

The aircraft floats motionless.

Sam trembles, "Oh my God. Oh my God."

"Why aren't they coming out?" Jeanie tosses a bucket over, "You think anybody's in there?"

"They coulda been killed hitting the water like that." Sam guesses, "if they were alive in the first place."

By now Irene has taken gazes in between buckets.

Suddenly a metal bar crashes out of the windshield of the gleaming, white-tiled, winged object. Another is used to scrape away the glass and two humanlike figures climb out.

Eddie sighs under his breath, "Two arks."

One of the human figures sheds what looks like a space suit and swims over to the ark. Jeanie tosses him a line. The other figure, lighter than water, floats around the craft in its suit, apparently working on the exterior, it's large globelike helmet bobbing about. By now, the first figure has approached close enough for all arksmen to see he's obviously human. A tall black man in top physical condition climbs on board Eddie's ark. Removing his soaked shirt, he pauses for a moment, hands on knees, catching his breath.

Irene drops her bucket and her jaw.

Eddie turns his head to Irene, "You can see him?"

Irene smiles, "Oh, yes!"

Deep breath, "Permission to board, sir," the polite stranger finally requests.

Eddie scoffs, "I was about to ask you the same thing."

The bent wet young man angles a confused eyebrow, "Sir?"

Eddie says nothing, confident that this pilot is sharp enough to put two and two together. The man, having filled his gut with air, stands erect and gives the boat a look around. Irene with the bucket and Jeanie dumping it over the railing, then Sam at the manual pump -- the stranger is no rocket scientist, but (well maybe he is), he gets the picture, "Oh my God, the only damned vessel on the face of the planet and it's sinking."

Eddie points at the plane, "Pardon me, but I see two vessels."

The man looks over too, "No, no. That one will float for another 10 minutes, tops, then it's on the ocean floor... Let me see your breach."

Eddie takes him down to the lower deck against the current of the bucket chain. David hops up as if he's seen a ghost, "Jesus Christ! Another person!"

Finally the man introduces himself, "Sorry, not Christ -- Lt. Major Kyle Taffort." Kyle jumps down into the pool of the lower deck with David. They shake.

"David Mac-something. Ark-hand... I don't know where the hell you came from, but," David fumbles giddily for his senses, "think you can fix this hole?"

Kyle dives under to get a better look. Eddie peeks down from beddeck.

David looks up at Eddie, "Eddie, what's goin' on?"

"Jesus, David, the friggin' space shuttle. These guys musta been trying ta wait out the storms in space."

"No shit?"

Kyle pops up, "I see your problem. The wood's too rotten to hold a screw. Let me get my partner and some materials..."

David's optimism resurfaces, "You can fix it?"

"I fix satellites all day. I should be able to fix your ... uhm ...ark?"

Eddie nods, "You and your partner -- are there more?"

"We'll have a lot to talk about captain, but first let's keep your craft above water." Kyle climbs up, jumps off and swims back to the floating shuttle. The bailing chain continues.

Irene catches Eddie, "Tell me he's coming back."

Eddie smiles, "Nah, he's coming back...And no, I didn't see a ring."

His rage completely forgotten, sucked from him as if by exorcism with the splash-diving shuttle, a noticeably more relaxed Eddie takes a check on Japer who is sleeping soundly. Eddie gently applies the cloth, "If you weren't up all last night I'd wake you for this Japer. You'd love it." Eddie

kisses Japer on the forehead and looks around one more time for the old man.

Kyle and partner work to salvage any useful items from the shuttle, swiftly loading various supplies, tools, cables, etc. onto two inflated rafts. The shuttle sinks slowly as they work, until it finally loses any semblance of buoyancy, the shuttle completely submerged but struggling to resist sinking, the two astronauts grabbing the last of their gear from a foot or so under the surface. An air pocket sharply breaks free, like a gasp, like the shuttle's last breath -- it lets go and sinks lifelessly toward the bottom of the ocean. Kyle flops his belly on the side of the raft, his hands in the water, he waves goodbye to his ship as it fades silently, peacefully below. Kyle's partner pats him on the head and the two maneuver their rafts back to Eddie Johnson's ark. Once docked, Kyle boards the ark, while his partner, still in full space suit, plunges into the water.

Kyle briefs Eddie. "My partner's got some tiling, on the outside. I'll get in there and stitch that wound right up."

One astronaut underwater breathing through hoses in the suit, one astronaut inside the ark's belly popping one-inch holes through the tiling and the hull, then stitching 3/4 inch cable around a 4x4-foot tile. Finally, they caulk the space between hole and cable from the outside, the caulk dries immediately. Kyle, down in lower deck, looks up with a smile.

David responds to the smile, "That's it? We won't sink?"

"Not only won't you sink," Kyle's smile expands, "but you won't burn up on re-entry, either."

The water level in the lower deck starts to decrease, and finally the coffee-grinders relax their efforts with a break.

Eddie puts down his bucket, "Let's pull your partner up."

With all hands up top, shuttle equipment littering the deck, Kyle flips the locks on his partner's mirror/sun-reflecting helmet. He gives it a quarter spin then pulls it up, revealing a crew-cut head and the face of a strong woman.

Eddie immediately grabs his chest and drops to one knee in disbelief, "Emily?" The word escapes his mouth like a tear from an eye, like the shuttle's last gasp.

Amused, Kyle turns to his partner. "You know this guy?"

The partner pauses with a long deep gaze toward Edward. "Yeah," she finally says calmly, "he's my husband."

"Your husband?"

Eddie's tears start up full force. "Emily!" But he's paralyzed by the sight of her.

Emily smiles some peaceful tears of her own and walks over to the frozen Eddie. She puts her arms around him. He passes out flat on his back. Everyone is just as dumfounded as when the shuttle hit the ocean.

Emily laughs, "Look at you, you old bear." She picks up the last bucket of lower deck water and splashes it on his face. Eddie coughs back to life. Emily leans down right on top of him. With both hands on his face, she grabs his scruffy beard and kisses Eddie's dehydrated lips, then looks up at Sam, who's stymied as well. "Sam!"

Sam runs over and hugs his mother. She's quite different-looking now, her wavy locks cut, heavy glasses gone, with a toned neck and cheek bones, and of course, that huge white suit eclipsing the rest of her body. But ten years later, even sweaty and red from the recent work out, Sam instantly recognizes his mother.

Irene looks over to Kyle. "Am I missing something here?"

Eddie, Sam and Emily quietly step down and pull back Japeth's canvas. They place Emily's helmet on his bed and watch him sleep. With Kyle up on deck telling space stories to the rest of the crew, the Johnson family snuggles on beddeck. Japeth opens his groggy eyes, the mirror glass helmet reflecting his own image. He stares for a while, assuming it's a fever dream. He gently strokes the glass with his finger.

Japeth pops up in sudden realization, "Where did this come from?!!!" he shouts out commandingly, having gained some strength during his brief sleep.

Eddie answers, "Your mother brought it."

Japeth's confusion only amplifies as he turns to see a new female face aboard the ark. The stranger moves in and hugs him. A mother and a son that have never met. Emily smiles and sheds a few tears. Japeth is still confused. His head on her shoulder he looks over at Eddie who smiles and nods like a child on his birthday.

"This is your mother, Japer." Eddie assures.

Japeth coughs up only bewilderment.

Sam is serious as a thunder storm. "That's mom, Japer, I swear to God."

The crew sits around the garage eating ravioli, both doors open.

Kyle debriefs. "So, we figured, O_2 down to just a couple a days for the five of us, a week's worth of rations, very little fuel. We had no choice but to try something desperate."

"So we drew straws. Kyle and I undocked the shuttle," Emily continues the story. "It took what little fuel we had left to break orbit, then we freefell back to ground ... I mean water."

"Could you see?" Eddie bumbles, "I mean from space, could you see if any ... land? You know."

"I'm sorry Eddie." Emily answers, "The cloud cover was so intense earlier on. The equipment had been down for the last two weeks. I mean, yeah, about three or four weeks ago, there were still mountain tops we knew about from satellite radar..."

Kyle nods, "And ground control, NASA, had moved to higher ground in the Appalachians, but we lost their signal twenty days ago."

"But that doesn't have to be because they're under," Japeth ever the optimist.

"That's right!" Emily encourages. "There's hundreds of reasons for communications loss...some of them ours. I mean the shuttle is not designed to stay in space that long."

David scratches his chin. "But coming in? As you fell in, did you see any land as you fell in?"

Kyle shakes his head. "No. No, but, our visuals were very limited and we weren't exactly lookin' out the window the whole time. And, well, despite the fact that we're very well trained, we don't land the shuttle -- seven computers do -- in practice. But this wasn't practice, and Emily and I had to do it ourselves -- and on water instead of a runway."

"Why didn't you break into a million pieces when you hit the water?" Japeth pops.

"Yep," Kyle pats Japeth on the head, "That's what I said when we were underwater. I mean, we did as good as possible a job with the angle of entry into the sea and that little parachute helped to slow us down, but it's still pretty damned amazing to me that that thing held together."

The group quietly nods in a tentative reflection, which Irene finally breaks, "And the others back in the space station?"

Emily turns to her, "We're supposed to find ground control. Tell them ISS's position. Or, more properly -- be seen by ground control."

"Well that hasn't exactly happened; we haven't located each other." Kyle finishes, "If that's still the case in a week, they're gonna jump too."

Japeth who's been folding a piece of paper, suddenly looks up. "Jump?"

"Not jump off the ISS," Emily explains. "Kyle means ... well there's a lifeboat, isn't that ironic? We call it a lifeboat -- the Russian Soyuz."

"It's a three-seater, which poses a problem." Kyle adds.

"So why didn't more of you come in the shuttle?" Eddie wonders out loud.

Kyle opens his hands up, "We didn't see you guys from space. We thought the trip down was more dangerous than staying up there. I mean, besides the very real possibility of smashing up on the water surface, we dropped into the atmosphere at an awkward angle. That is incredibly stupid. The entire craft isn't covered with tiles. But with little power -- we had no choice. But the shuttle, we thought, would be much easier to spot by ground control because of its size."

"It could have been much worse." Emily leans back. "You can't maneuver well in space without power. We pretty much fell into the atmosphere like a brick."

Jeanie, feeling like Eddie's much too happy about Emily being aboard to get upset over anything she has to say, relaxes her shut mouth quarantine, "So that was it? You just drew straws?"

"Something like that." Kyle chuckles, "Well, I lost -- or won. I was supposed to go alone. But Emily made a convincing argument about the other Soyuz being really crowded with four, and frankly insisted she ride with me." He looks over at Eddie like he's looking at a ghost, " I had no idea -- no idea she was -- Jesus -- your wife."

Eddie puts down his can of ravioli and sets his hands on Emily's shoulders.

David turns to Emily and clears his throat, "I don't mean to be insensitive, but Eddie said you died."

Emily smiles through watery eyes, "I did die."

Japeth finishes folding his paper in the shape of the space shuttle. He walks over to the stern and gives the paper a push. The paper shuttle finds flight in the fancy of the whirling wind behind the bobbing boat. Were there little paper astronauts inside, they could look in their little paper rearview mirror and see the "SS Emily" floating off into the twilight.

Sam holds a whimpering Jeanie in their bed area. "Maybe your mother is alive, too," Sam soothes sympathetically.

Jeanie can't stop her tears. "I'm sorry, Sam, I'm sorry. I should be happy for you. I really should be."

"No, I understand."

"No you don't! I mean, God!" Jeanie whimpers.

"That's just it. I mean ... I mean." Sam inhales, "You know, I never got into the whole God thing. You know, we all just kind of avoided Henry. You know."

"I know. I know. I didn't either. I didn't either, but I couldn't avoid it."

"I'm saying, what I'm saying is, I think you'll agree -- that there really seems ta be a god now. I mean, my dad goin' nuts, this boat and rain." Sam pounds his palm to the wooden deck and points out the porthole.

"And your mother."

"That's it. That's it exactly. I mean, I believed there was a god at first. I mean, you know, my dad tells me it's gonna rain and we gotta build an ark. I was like your folks. I was like...*right Dad.* But then I believed him when I saw the

rain. When I saw all that rain I got scared. I believed because I didn't want to die."

"So?"

"So? So... that's so lame. I mean, what a wimp! I mean, I couldn't believe there was a god for any better reason than I was scared to die? ...And then, and then, after I knew Arlington was under. After we looked out for days and all we could see was more rain and water, not even a bird in the sky. I knew, absolutely knew there was a god, and he was pissed. And I was pissed too."

"You too, huh?"

"I was in shock. You know, I was confused. But inside, I knew there was a god. And I knew he took my mother, and Henry and your family too."

"And you thought... you thought...he is not a good god."

Sam's eyes start to water, but he's determined to get this out, "Yeah. Yeah. I thought that. And the only thing I could do to stay halfway sane was to forget about all that and just survive."

Jeanie begins to rock back and forth, "Me too."

"But now. Now. Now my mother. This is crazy. A bad god -- why would he do that? I mean not for me. I barely remember her. To be honest, I'm more scared having a mom now than not. But Dad, Dad never forgot her. You just have no idea what a gift this is for my dad. Why would a bad god do that?"

Sam sighs and Jeanie rocks.

"Knock, Knock," They hear Eddie's voice from behind their canvas.

Sam takes a second to return to reality. He pulls the canvas back, revealing a smiling Eddie.

"Yeah?" Sam asks unenthusiastically.

"You decent?" Eddie asks.

Sammy and Jeanie look matter-of-factly at themselves, "Yeah."

"Good!" Eddie claws at a nail slightly bent in the wood, "Er, ah, son. Rumor has it, you have access to, uhm..."

Eddie's "uhm" falls off into an awkward silence. He can build an ark in the middle of Columbus, then keep it afloat with nearly only his own will, but to ask his son for condoms simply stymies him.

Jeanie, uncharacteristically, takes the opportunity to help him through. "Ah, Sam, I think he wants the condoms."

"That's right," Eddie nods, "what she said."

Sam sighs, "Why are you coming to me? David's been diggin' at them in lower deck, over the squirrels, just by the gauze."

"Oh, sure, thanks." But before rushing off, Eddie delays his indulgence for a few kind words to his son. "Thank you, son. Did I tell you, I'm so proud of you?"

"Yes, Dad."

"And that I love you."

"Yes, Dad."

"And your mother loves you too."

"Dad!" Sam is uncomfortable enough with his giddy father breathing over him after such an intense conversation. "Go do … the thing! It's been ten years!"

"And how long has it been for you?"

Sam stops in surprise.

"He's a gentleman, Mr. Johnson." Jeanie answers.

Eddie smiles and backs out leaving Sam feeling even more awkward. Jeanie cracks the dried tears on her face with a peaceful smile, "A real gentleman."

Sam's eyes widen, "Really?"

Jeanie's smile turns to a laugh.

Japeth, no longer under the weather, changes Sheila's diaper. "So it looks like I've got a mommy too now. You're not the only one."

Sheila stares up at the ceiling.

Japeth powders her bottom. "I never had a mommy and now I do. Just like that. No mommy, then mommy." He safety pins a clean diaper on. "So what do I do? I've got two parents. I mean, I'm not complaining. I think I'm happy. I think. It's just weird. No mommy. Mommy."

Under the water, two dolphins swim side by side, playfully flirting. They hear the muffled pants and sighs of three couples making love. The dolphins charge the surface of the water. Leaping skyward, they glean a bright star swiftly tracking -- the International Space Station helplessly spinning. Two shooting stars dart off in another corner of the night sky. A shimmering flash, and the edge of the aurora.

Midnight. What a day journal! What a day. We're just about down for the count, then the freaking space shutle -- the goddam space shutle -- can you believe that! Drops right out of the sky -- and if that isn't crazy enough, who walks out but Eddie's late wife. Yeah, Eddie's survived that whack to the head and this flood, but I thought the site of Emily was going to stop his heart right there. He deserved it though. Emily coming back. I didn't even stop to think of that when I saw Sue.

Day *64*

In the silver-blue pre-dawn light, Jeanie sits cross-legged up in the crow's nest improvising on the flute, a cougar in her lap, the melody playing in waves. Sam climbs to the top of the pole to join her. The sun peeks up over the horizon. Sam listens patiently. Jeanie finishes her melody and takes the flute from her lips.

Sam lays his hand on her head, "Are you okay?"

"I'm happy to be alive, Sam."

Sam nods.

Jeanie looks out over the waters at the orange morning sun, "I'm happy I'm alive."

The sun, as if to agree, seems to speed its ascent, but in an eerily unnatural arc, peaks at twenty degrees above the horizon and drops down just as fast. Twilight, then stars.

"Did you see that?" Sam's eyes search for the bashful sun.

"The sun set the second it came out."

"What is that? What is that?"

"Maybe we're way north like in Alaska?"

"But Japeth said..."

Just then a military plane whizzes over head, but it's somehow translucent. Surreal, it starts dropping bombs all around the little ark. They don't hit the ark, but explode nearby, waking everyone. The couples look out of their portholes in terror. Kyle and Irene, in the garage, open one of the big doors. The plane is gone as fast as it came. Underwater shrapnel pocks the underside of the boat, causing many thousands of tiny little leaks. The explosions push up clouds of moisture from the waters. The clouds wisp into forms, apparitions of condensation, vapor ghosts. In one haze of figures a man kills his wife with a can opener. In

other misty scenes: a gang rape, a driveby shooting, car bombs. The heinous acts continue and escalate.

Sam and Jeanie hold each other tightly in fear. The short wave radio flickers and comes to life. A crusty signal crackles ...

Newscaster: "and stuffed her own baby in a dumpster around back. The child born addicted to crack cocaine has been taken under...**click** ...declared war....**click** ... opened fire on the hundreds still boarded up in the church. At this time there are no survivors...beat his wife into a coma...lied to his friend ... stole from her mother ... ignored his child ... didn't love his ..."

Radio show host: "So Julie, you knew Roland loves you and wanted to marry you. Why would you cheat on him?"

Radio Julie: "Geeze, cheat is such a harsh word. It wasn't like that. I mean, I just had to get this wild side out, you know."

Radio JJ's voice: "Christ! We stunk the place up, didn't we?"

Radio God's voice: "Be good my children. Tomorrow is a new day. Let us rejoice and be glad in it. ... *please.*"

The ark passengers peer through the portholes. The horrendous acts become more intense until the sun begins to rise once again -- this time vertically. The sun's rays burn up the moisture of the ghosts; they die evaporative deaths. The heavy drops fall into the waters. Weeping stars disappear and a golden rainbow appears in the west. Sam points at it as everyone comes up on deck, save for Irene, who climbs down to check on the animals.

"It's Golden!" Jeanie bursts.

"The whole rainbow is gold." Sue is amazed.

Eddie's body is battling a mixture of emotions and one of them is anger. Anger over the new leaks, anger over

the whole rainbow/promise thing. Nonetheless, he still looks out at this rainbow a little differently.

David bitterly referring to the apparitions, "What the hell was all that?"

"It can't be a rainbow." Kyle shields his eyes from the sun. "I mean it shouldn't appear to be getting closer as we drift towards it."

The huge golden band glimmers in the sunrise. Japeth takes Emily by the hand. "Up in the space station, did you know your position?"

"Yes, we still had pen and paper."

"We're over the United States, right? Maybe somewhere in the Midwest." Japeth begins to poke at a thought.

Emily raises an eyebrow at her young son's intelligent guess, "Southern Illinois."

"Or eastern Missouri," he corrects her.

Emily's eyes widen with the realization of Japeth's plan, "Japeth ... I'm so proud of you!"

Kyle is on to it as well, "Quick get the cables!"

Kyle and Emily race to the cables, punching holes in the main board with the shuttle's special tools.

Sue pokes, too. "What? What is it?"

Kyle, working fiercely, "That's no rainbow. It keeps getting closer."

David finally forgets the water spray attack, tilts his head at the gold rainbow. "Yeah, why is that?"

Eddie, "Doesn't look like gold to me."

"More like stainless steel, huh?" Kyle finishes knotting the cable to the ship's bow, "We're drifting right towards it. If we can mount these cables to your boat, we'll be able to anchor to it."

"Anchor to what?!!!" Eddie bursts.

With his right hand still in Emily's left, Japeth takes his father's hand with the other. "St. Louis, Dad. It's the tip of St. Louis arch."

Jeanie relaxes and smiles.

"No way!" David chuckles in disbelief, "The damn St. Louis arch!"

Eddie marvels for a second at the glimmering, now-silvery band quickly approaching. "And the plane? The ghosts?"

"You're the prophet, Captain," Kyle returns. "You tell us."

Eddie, yet again, doesn't know. He shakes his head as he stares.

Emily steps in. "A reminder?"

Kyle, finished fastening the other end of the cable to a small secondary anchor, readies. "Okay, we're gonna only have one shot at this. Anyone think they can lasso a rainbow?"

Kyle looks around at the dumbfounded crew. Finally David raises his hand. "I'll do it. I mean, I'll try, unless someone here used to rope goats or somethin'."

Kyle hands David the cable and anchor. "I grew up in the Bronx, man. Never even seen a goat."

David walks up on top of the garage into the crow's nest to mount his feet. Jeanie and Sam step down to deck. The small boat drifts toward the right leg of the St. Louis Arch, David swinging the cable around like a cowboy.

Kyle cups his hands around his mouth and yells to anyone with arms, "When it swings around, one of us is gonna have to grab it and clamp it down!"

The water level has submerged all but thirty feet of the St. Louis Arch. Its water-beaded tip reflecting the sun in sharp rays of steel-golden white light. Eddie's ark drifts just to the right of the right leg.

"NOW!" Kyle shouts.

David lets loose. The cable whips around the leg just as they pass. The rubber-coated anchor elbows out at its end and back to the little ship. As if looking for him specifically, it skates right into Sam's chest -- a three-point horseshoe ringer. He grabs it with both arms and falls flat on his back, sliding another six feet.

"Great catch Sammer!" David yells down.

"Are you okay?" Jeanie runs over.

In a rush, Kyle has already retrieved and untied the anchor and clamped the cable back down to the bow. "Hold on to something!"

The boat continues its lazy waft, driftwood. The cable stretches to taut and, anchored by the radiant arch, it suddenly jerks the ark to a stop. A pure, low perfect 'A' tone cna almost be heard as inertia topples everyone onboard like unsuspecting wine glasses under a poorly drawn tablecloth from some inept magician. The cable flicks under David's left foot. He trips forward with his head into the pole ladder. Then, unconscious, he flies limp from the crow's nest over Emily, his back arched as if leaning to balance a sailboat. The shocked crewmembers look up from their tumble, time seems to hold David like a feather as he drifts overhead. Kyle, head cocked back, reaches up with one strong arm and grabs David by the shirt on his way overboard.

"David!" Sue shrieks.

Kyle pulls David down on top deck and pats his cheek, "Yippee Yi Yo, cowboy." Kyle lowers his ear to David's mouth, puts two fingers to his neck, "He's breathing, strong pulse."

Sue jumps over and grabs her ears in shock, "David? David?"

David dizzily reaches up to rub the bruise pulsing on his forehead, "Whoa! We got it!"

Sue kisses David, takes a relaxing deep breath, then kisses Kyle on the forehead, "Thank you!"

"Yeah, Mac-something, keen ropin'," Kyle assures.

David rubs his head, "How long was I out?"

"About an hour and a half," Kyle jokes, "Breathing, but no pulse."

"Breathing, but no pulse?" David cracks his neck, "I didn't know that was possible."

"Shouldn't be," Emily smiles with her eyes.

David grabs his heart, then tries to check his own pulse.

"They're yankin' you buddy. You were just out for a second," rubbing his hand on David's head, Eddie shows some mercy, " Bet you saw a few stars though."

The current is not perfectly perpendicular to the arch so the boat drags at an angle favoring the interior of the arch.

"Kyle, look at the color variations on the steel." Emily steals attention away from David.

Eddie turns his head, "What? What?"

Kyle looks over, noticing yet another thing, "The water level is dropping -- and pretty fast I think."

"Faster than we're sinking?" Eddie wonders out loud.

Kyle holds up his thumb like a painter.

Eddie gives his question another airing, "What? What?"

"I don't know yet," Kyle lowers his thumb, "but just in case let's get the other cable mounted on the backa this thing."

Emily and Kyle begin the process again of mounting the cable, this time to the other end of the boat.

"The current is being friendly." Emily notes.

Eddie tired of asking for clarification, Sammy picks up. "What's happening?"

Irene, panting, pops up from the hatch, a cougar under each arm, "It's filling up fast down there, the lower deck is completely under. I've got the animals on beddeck, but I think that'll be full too pretty darned soon." She calms

in bewilderment at the magnificently stable arch and the cable holding the ship to it, "Uhm, shouldn't we use that caulking stuff or something?"

Kyle doesn't look up from his work, "We barely had enough for the earlier repairs." He finishes a clamp, leaves the mounting to Emily, and runs back to the other end of deck to do the thumb thing again. "Anyway if we can't lasso that other leg, we'll be hanging upside-down, probably sooner."

Eddie tilts his head, squinting down the line of Kyle's thumb. "How's it look?"

Kyle smiles facetiously, "Two thumbs up!"

Eddie doesn't catch the joke, "That's good, right?"

"The first time the cable was one thumb up the arch, above the water line. Now, it's two thumbs up, you do the math." Kyle catches Emily's signal that the mounting routine is finished, she hands him the second cable. He climbs up to the crow's nest and lassos the left leg of the arch with much greater ease this time as the boat is no longer adrift. Sam grabs the anchor and keeps his feet on the ground. Kyle pops down and mounts the cable to the stern.

Emily assists, "Now, as the water level drops. The ark won't. It'll just hang here like a kid hanging from monkey bars, draining. That's why we had to anchor twice to the, to the, uhm, rainbow."

Still flustered, "We would have sunk," Irene exhales.

"Don't know if the ark can take the stress, so," Kyle stands back to his feet, still in mission mode, "with one more cable we'll be able to climb up and into the arch."

Eddie scratches his head, "You can get inside that thing?"

"Yeah, yeah." David fills in, "There's a little space up there for tourists. Didn't you see the windows?"

Eddie cracks his head up at the arch, now only ten or twenty feet above him and to the sides.

"But the windows look too small," Jeanie worries.

"Then we'll get on top and see if we can remove one of those steel panels." The ever-ready Kyle figures.

Eddie takes his eye off the golden steel for a second, "And then how will we get down ... I mean, once the waters run off or whatever?"

"There's like a cable car in the legs." David points out.

Kyle nods, "And if that's not operational -- which it probably ain't, we can climb down its cable."

Invisible to the hardworking crew of the SS Emily, the international space station makes a pass above the blue planet. Huge billowing gray clouds still blanket portions of the planet. Floating like giant pillows, they slowly whiten, slowly wane.

Having climbed up from the shrapnel-ridden, wood-rotting, roach-infested vessel, all sit atop the arch as water drains from the bottom of the boat like a bowl of water-boiled pasta in a strainer. Mist still spraying from shrapnel holes, a NASA shuttle tile sown to its side shouts in a heavy contrast of technologies, like a TV in a teepee.

Lying on her back, Jeanie starts. "I'm scared I might slide off of this thing, but I'm too tired to do anything about it."

Japeth crawls over, "I'm the smallest, it's easiest for me to move around. I'll get the rope." Japeth scurries over the bellies of the panting rainbow captures, tying them together with the last of the plastic rope.

"Good..." Eddie mutters, too tired to finish his thought.

Like fish stranded on the rocks, they squint up at the sun.

"After all that rain, I can't believe I'm saying this, but that sun is gonna fry us in an hour or so," a parched-lip Sue warns.

"Wake me up if I catch fire," Kyle's last word burns slowly off his tongue as he falls fast asleep in the heated rays.

"What about the animals?" Irene's brain being more active than her body.

Emily's eyes slowly squint closed, "They should nap too."

Irene struggles to keep herself motivated, "Shouldn't we pull them up?"

Eddie's snores answer.

"Probably," David mumbles as he slips into slumber.

Irene rolls her head and peers down at the ark. The two cougars peer up expectantly. She whispers, "Don't worry, we'll be back for you my lovelies -- we just need a second to catch our..." And Irene joins the rest in the magnetic attraction of sleep. Heavy and tired, as if the sun itself were resting on their bellies, the crew falls into a deep, sunburnt sleep. The cougars, too, lay their heads over their paws and close their eyes.

Breathing, but no pulse. They thought they were joking, but they nailed me right on the head. That is so funny. Breathing, but no pulse., can you believe it? I'm sitting on top of the freakin St Luis Arch. What a day! I got knocked out. But we lassued a rainbow. That's funny. Breathing, but no pulse, then I lassued a rainbow.

Anyway, they're all asleep. Sleeping on the top of this arch, the waterlevel dropping. Sheila in Sue's arms. I woke up and was just staring at her ... she's so little, so fresh , so very very innocent. You make love to a woman and less than a year later, a baby. It's a miracle flat out. I mean, we all were pretty flord with Emily -- I guess resurrecting or whatever -- I don't quite get it. I guess you got to call that a miracle. But, I don't know. Just looking at Sheila -- I think that's even more amaizing. I messed up a few things in my life, and Sue, I love her, but she's no saint neither. Still, the two of us, we can make such a beautiful innocent life -- with a clean slate. Sheila's clean slate -- I'm going to do my damdest to raise her to be better than me, a better person. but in the end its her ball game. Anyway, a whole life where none was there before, thats a miracle. I mean, at least like Emily was there before. Anyway, she seems nice, Emily that is, no wonder Eddie kept that torch going.

Kyle wakes with a nagging thought. "So, I don't get it."

Emily rolls her head toward Kyle. "Get what?"

"Well, let's start with you. I've known you for two years and you never mentioned Eddie."

"I told you I was married."

"Yeah, yeah, but you never introduced us, you never... you just kept your whole family secret. And why wouldn't you have gone to visit 'em? How did you ...? I mean where did you come from? Just reincarnated two years ago?

God zap astronaut memory pack into your skull or something?"

"I'm not saying I can explain it either. But, look at this planet, Kyle, filled with water up to the mountaintops. Does this make sense to you? There's not enough water in the entire weather system to do this -- that ever cross your mind?"

"Well, yes, I'm impressed," Kyle nods. "Hey, but what about all that underground water we don't know about."

"Come on, Taffort. Even if there was enough of that, the pressure needed to get all that water out of the ground and into the air would raise atmospheric temperatures to scorching levels. Everything would be boiled beyond recognition."

Kyle nods again, "So you're gonna just chalk it up to *miracle*?"

"I will if you will."

Kyle rolls his eyes.

"That's an awful suspicious look on your face," Emily reclines her head back to resting position, "for someone sitting on the top of a golden rainbow."

Kyle only sighs, "It's stainless steel!"

Japeth peers upward, then points at the sky... "Another plane!"

Irene's eyes open, "No more bombs...please."

"No, a real plane!" Japeth continues his point.

Sam squints, "You mean, a real helicopter."

"Yeah!" Japeth smiles, "Yeah!"

The kayak paddle-like propeller, with all the irony of sun-dried storm-troopers, mimics the sound of a fisherman's outboard motor. Irene grips the steel arch, looking up from her cat-kneeling position. The vibrating airwaves amplify. Belly up on the arch, their eyes open like rose petals in a field of tall grass. The helicopter hovers heavenly, two bright orange fuel tanks squeezing either side of it, gleaming like

suns. The sound, the intense orange, are hypnotizing. A bull-horned voice, louder than God, breaks out over the waves: "Majors Taffort and Johnson?"

Kyle and Emily lazily sit up and informally salute.

Emily mumbles to Kyle, "They must have sighted us at re-entry."

Eddie's jaw drops, "My God, there are others alive!"

The bullhorn bellows again, "Mr. Edward Johnson?"

Eddie's jaw slams shut. Confused and uncertain as to how to respond, he decides to copy Kyle and Emily. He awkwardly leans up and uncomfortably salutes.

The helicopter steadies, hovering just ten feet from the crew which dangles atop the St. Louis Arch, the bullhorn voice howls, "Jesus Christ, your son wasn't pulling our legs."

Eddie reaches out with his right hand and grabs his chest. Emily grabs Eddie's other hand, a tad worried that he might faint.

"Soldiers, we're too far out. We don't have the fuel to hover any longer, but we'll send out some crews as the waters recede. Right now, we only have space for the two majors."

Sheila wakes herself into a good healthy cry. David slides his journal into the back of his pants and picks up the naked screaming child. He kisses her with a few tears in his eyes. "It's gonna be so different for you Sheila."

"David?" Sue wakes to the sight of this mechanical hummingbird.

Inside the chopper, the pilot's palm covers the microphone which is in the hands of a decorated colonel. "If they've really been floating out here sir, they probably won't know..."

The colonel nods and pats the pilot on the knee. He pulls the microphone back to his mouth, "A huge natural

disaster, ladies and gentlemen, but not a one casualty known to me at this time."

Jeanie cuddles her arms around Sam and kisses the back of his neck.

"Just a lot of crowded mountain tops. From Chicago to Tokyo, and all the way around, a hell of a lot of people crammin' mountains worldwide." The colonel continues, "Like they said, we moved to 'higher ground.'"

Eddie lowers his head, scratches his beard, and mutters under his breath, "You kept your promise." His one good eye wells up. "You really kept your promise."

"Really, Mr. Johnson? An ark in an arch?" The bullhorn scowls.

Emily wets her dry lips and kisses Eddie's burly cheek. "Guess he was just bluffin'."

The chopper lowers a line; Kyle grabs hold and winches up. Irene and David wave a hand to him. As Kyle rises, he smiles back. "Look up Eddie! All that faith has brought you an angel."

Emily nods in agreement. "Eddie, you go. I'll stay with the kids." She whispers into Eddie's ear, "Say 'hello' to Henry for me."

With Kyle on the chopper, the line lowers a second time. Eddie clutches it like a child grips the thumb of its father. Twisted wire never felt so good. All his weight on his arms, Eddie's feet enjoy a flying sense of zero gravity. He watches the helicopter near; it's as if he's being pulled into the sun itself. Kyle's hand appears out of a beam of glaring light. Eddie grabs hold and climbs aboard. He sighs stupidly and looks back down at the arch. Above his decaying boat, every weary crewmember rises to their feet.

A teary-eyed Eddie wipes his face with his big hands, then turns his head again out the window to wave back at the worn group atop the arch. Each of them stands erect, firm, straight hands at their foreheads, passionately saluting, the

sun reflecting off their eyes, off the water. The cougars, too, squint upward.

The chopper drifts left and away. Eddie trembles a smile, sniffs up a few tears, waves gently with bewildered eyes until the curve of statuesque saluters can no longer be seen over the curve of the oceans. Eddie sits back in position and stares simply forward. Kyle seat-belts him and grabs a clipboard from a hook on the side wall, marks a few numbers, makes a few sketches, begins a debriefing to the colonel concerning the recent space station operations. The colonel, however, ignores Kyle completely; he's had his eyes glued to Eddie Johnson the entire time. Finally, Eddie realizes the Colonel's presence. Their eyes connect. The Colonel dons an unbelieving smile and casts Eddie a powerful salute. Eddie relaxes back and chuckles. The colonel smiles, sighs, then turns toward Kyle's clipboard. He picks up the microphone muttering off coordinates to ground control making sure they understand that he has "the" Eddie Johnson onboard.

Eddie gazes out the opposite window at all the water; no end to it, just shimmering blue waves and an apathetic horizon. A bird's eye view, but the speed is dizzying, he again dozes off with exhaustion.

A tap on the shoulder wakes him some hours later. He rubs his eye, unclasps his seat belt and throws his hands onto the window. The tips of the Appalachian Mountains peak out of the water like islands. Covered with makeshift shelters, wood and corrugated aluminum, the small patches of land are crammed with people. From tree to tree -- shoulder to shoulder -- people; a green jagged ridge simply teaming with people. Eddie stares down on the heads of masses. They pock the mountainsides now like millions upon millions of raindrops had pelted the sea.

In an extremely tight clearing, the chopper lands. Kyle and the Colonel rise to their feet, allowing Eddie to step

out first. Eddie stumbles slowly to the ground. He pauses, looking down at the earth between his feet, enjoying the incredibly inconceivably steadying pleasure of firm footing. Too overcome to move, Eddie's eye locks on his two feet -- solid ground beneath them. Solid ground. Like iron must feel to magnets. He's frozen in the gravity of the moment. The helicopter's gyrating propeller calms to a hum. Even the bustling crowd -- people climbing over people to get a look at Eddie -- even they calm to a hush at the sight of this big man, locked in a lowered head stance with solid ground.

Kyle steps out after him. "Eddie? … Eddie?"

Eddie takes no notice.

Finally, Henry, swimming his way through the gawking masses, reaches to break Eddie's deadlock. "Dad?"

"Henry?" Eddie slowly brings his head up from the stupor. Tears whirlpooling in his eyes, Eddie bear hugs his eldest son. They clamp together with all the strength of Earth's gravity. The helicopter's propellers finally come to a complete rest. Thousands of pigeons, perhaps tens of thousands, flock to the tree branches surrounding the landing area. They fill the light blue sky like snow, like confetti, like a shower of motherly kisses. Henry and Eddie hug like koalas, cry like babies, refusing to break their hold through the storm of raining applause from a displaced mountainful of you and me.

The End

First hand David MacMay,

Well, look at us, we finally landed, finally made it to the "higher ground" that Jeanie and Eddie hoped was really there. We were all worried about ourselves, but Eddie was all worried about all of them in the flood, not just Henry, but all of them. Even with God on his side. That's funny. Eddie believed in God and I believed in Eddie. Anyway, Everyone here is all talking about Eddie's ark. Eddie Johnson's Ark. The cornal took a picture of the ark in that "rainbow." It's so falling apart, I can't believe we actually survived on that thing as long as we did. Everyday was an adventure. It's pretty amaizing. It's amaizing to see those people look at that photo. I mean they're impressed and all, but they're confused too. Half of em say, "Why'd he bild an ark in the first playce, when he couldve just climbed the mountain like us?" I hear that a lot "even if God did talk to Eddie ... what was the point? Huh? What was the point? As long as we all didn't get killed?" That's what they say, as if it wouldve all made sense if they were to have drown to death.

Actually, alot of em are still confused it didn't happen that way. if they don't see it - then maybe it really was pointless. Shit, maybe I just got a better point of view on the ark. Waking up alive. Each new day. I mean, I think everyday, every single fuckin day is a miracle like Sheila is a miracle. Every day is probly God himself or herself or whatever, asking everybody to bild an ark, to rescue what is good in our lives in our hearts in our heads.

Anyway, I can't really say I know God, I only know him threw Eddie. but I do know me, and how I can be me doing good or bad stuff. Or even just passing up good when I know for a fact its staring me in the face. Everyday, I know the choice is there for me to either bild a fucking ark, or run up the side of a mountain and hide. Drag my life up a mountain as if its worth saving. "Why did Eddie waste his time bilding an ark? He put hisself and family in more danger than us in the flood?" ... Breathing, but no pulse. I've had enough of running up mountains.